THE ALPHA'S REJECTED DESTINY

NORIKO KIYOSHI

© 2024 Noriko Kiyoshi. All rights reserved. No part of this book may be reproduced, stored in a retrieval system, or transmitted in any form or by any means, electronic, mechanical, photocopying, recording, or otherwise, without prior written permission of the publisher, except for brief quotations used in critical reviews or articles. This is a work of fiction. Any resemblance to actual events or persons, living or dead, is purely coincidental.

Dedication

To the readers who believe in the power of love, fate, and second chances—this one is for you. Thank you for joining me on this journey. May you always find the courage to follow your heart, no matter where it leads.

With love,
Noriko Kiyoshi

PREFACE

Under the silver gaze of the Moon Goddess, every soul has a destined match—a bond stronger than blood, more eternal than the stars. For werewolves, this connection is sacred, a guiding force meant to unite hearts and strengthen packs. It is said that when mates meet, the universe itself holds its breath, and for one fleeting moment, everything feels perfectly aligned.
But what happens when the bond is denied?
For Alpha Caelan Thorn, the weight of destiny clashed with the pull of his own desires. When he first locked eyes with Selene Duskwood, his fated mate, he felt the magnetic tether between them, but instead of embracing it, he turned away. She was quiet and unassuming, a shadow in his world of dominance and command. He craved something different—something bold, exciting, and human.
Felicity Carter was everything Selene was not. A fiery force of nature with no ties to the werewolf world, she dazzled him with her confidence and ambition. In her, he thought he had found what he truly wanted, rejecting the bond that tied him to Selene.
But the heart and destiny are stubborn things.
This is the story of a choice, a rejection, and the journey back to what was always meant to be. It is a tale of love and betrayal, of strength and redemption, and of the undeniable power of a mate bond.
The Moon never lies. And for Alpha Caelan, it would take jealousy, heartbreak, and the threat of losing everything to learn what he should have known from the start:
A true Alpha always stands by his destined mate.
And yet, destiny does not easily forgive those who defy its plans.
Selene, heartbroken but resilient, vowed to survive the rejection, even as the threads of the mate bond lingered like a ghost, refusing to release her completely. She stayed in the pack not out of weakness but out of strength, determined to

carve a place for herself where she would no longer be defined by the sting of Caelan's choice.

Felicity, on the other hand, had no interest in the traditions of wolves or the sacred customs of their world. What she craved was power—power over Caelan, power over the pack, and the thrill of bending the rules to suit her desires. To her, Selene was an obstacle, an inconvenience to be eliminated, no matter the cost.

As their paths collided and the dynamics within the pack shifted, Caelan began to see the cracks in the perfect image of the human woman he had chosen. And when another wolf's eyes lingered on Selene a little too long—when another man dared to see the worth he had overlooked—Caelan's instincts roared to life, shaking his conviction to its core.

In this journey, alliances will be tested, enemies will rise, and love will burn brighter than the most radiant moon. Because in the end, no one can truly escape their destiny—not even an Alpha.

Selene and Caelan's story begins with rejection.
But it ends with a choice.

CHAPTER 1: THE REJECTION

The full moon hung low in the sky, bathing the clearing in a silvery glow. The pack had gathered beneath the ancient oaks, their breaths steaming in the crisp night air as the annual Moonlit Ceremony began. It was a sacred tradition, a time when the Moon Goddess revealed the destinies of her children and united mates under her eternal light.

Alpha Caelan Thorn stood at the center of the gathering, his broad shoulders squared and his piercing blue eyes scanning the crowd. Power radiated off him in waves, his presence commanding respect, and not a single wolf dared meet his gaze for long. His jet-black hair, tousled by the cool breeze, only added to the allure that made him the perfect leader.

The pack waited, hushed and reverent, as the ceremony began. Wolves from all ranks stood shoulder to shoulder, anticipating the mystical moment when the Moon's power would guide their souls to their destined mates. Caelan, however, felt a knot of impatience twisting in his chest. He didn't want this.

The idea of surrendering to fate—of giving up control to some unseen force—grated against everything he stood for as an Alpha. He prided himself on forging his own path, making his own choices. But tradition demanded his presence, and so here he was, enduring it.

A flicker of movement caught his attention. From the edge of the crowd stepped Selene Duskwood, her dark hair falling in soft waves around her face. Her forest-green eyes darted nervously around the gathered wolves, and she hugged herself as though the night's chill seeped deeper into her skin than anyone else's.

She was unassuming, quiet, and ordinary—a she-wolf who blended into the background. Nothing about her screamed Alpha's mate, and yet, when their eyes met across the clearing, everything shifted.

Caelan froze.

It hit him like a bolt of lightning, an overwhelming pull that left him momentarily breathless. His wolf stirred within him, growling with recognition. Mate. The word echoed in his mind, powerful and inescapable.

Selene's lips parted in surprise, and he saw the same realization dawning in her wide eyes. Her steps faltered, but she continued forward, the bond already working its magic, drawing them together like two halves of the same soul.

For a moment, the world stopped. The murmurs of the pack faded into silence, the rustling trees seemed to still, and all that remained was the connection between them—a force so primal and raw that it left no room for doubt.

And then Caelan did the unthinkable.

He turned away.

"I reject her," he said, his voice strong and clear, cutting through the stillness like a blade.

A collective gasp rippled through the crowd. Even the Beta, Astrid, a fierce warrior and Caelan's closest advisor, widened her eyes in shock. The rejection was not unheard of but was rare enough to cause scandal, especially coming from an Alpha.

Selene staggered, her expression crumbling. "What?" she whispered, her voice barely audible over the pounding in her ears.

Caelan forced himself to meet her gaze, his jaw tightening. He had to do this. For himself. For the pack. "I don't accept this bond," he said, each word deliberate and heavy. "You're not the mate I choose."

Her heartbreak was palpable, written in the way her shoulders slumped and her hands clenched at her sides. The pack watched in stunned silence as Selene, too stunned to respond, simply turned and walked away, disappearing into the shadows of the forest.

Caelan exhaled slowly, ignoring the weight of the pack's eyes on him. He could feel their confusion, their disapproval, but he had made his choice.

From the edge of the gathering, another figure approached. Felicity Carter, a striking human woman with fiery red hair and sharp, confident features, sauntered into the clearing. She moved with the ease of someone who commanded attention and thrived in the spotlight.

"Was that necessary?" she asked, her lips curving into a teasing smile as she looped her arm through his.

"Completely," Caelan replied, his voice steady even as his wolf growled in protest deep within him.

He felt the sting of the bond breaking, the ache that came from rejecting something so fundamental, but he shoved it aside. Felicity represented a future he could control—a choice he could own.

As the ceremony ended and the pack dispersed, Caelan couldn't help but glance once toward the trees where Selene had vanished.

For the briefest of moments, he felt something—guilt, doubt, maybe even regret. But he pushed it down, burying it beneath the certainty of his decision.

This was his path now. And there was no turning back.

CHAPTER 2: SELENE'S RESOLVE

The forest was her sanctuary.
Selene ran through the trees, her breaths sharp and ragged, her chest aching as much from the emotional blow as from the cold night air. The towering pines blurred past her, and the soft earth cushioned her bare feet. She wanted to scream, to cry, to rage at the Moon Goddess for what had just happened, but no sound escaped her lips. Only silence.
When she finally stopped, she collapsed against a tree trunk, her fingers gripping the rough bark. The moonlight filtered through the canopy above, illuminating her tear-streaked face. The Moon Goddess had chosen her for him. For Caelan. And he had rejected her.
A dull ache spread through her chest, not just from heartbreak but from the mate bond itself. It was fraying now, unraveling like an old threadbare fabric. She felt the absence like a hollow space in her soul, and the pain was excruciating. She pressed a hand to her heart, willing herself to breathe.
"Get up," she whispered to herself, her voice shaking. "This doesn't define you. He doesn't define you."
Selene had spent her life as a shadow in the pack, overlooked and underestimated. She wasn't a warrior, not like Astrid or the other fierce she-wolves. She wasn't a charmer, nor did she command attention with confidence like Felicity. But she was still a wolf, still part of this pack, and she refused to let this rejection destroy her.
Pushing herself to her feet, she wiped her tears with the back of her hand and took a steadying breath.
"I'll make him see what he gave up," she murmured. "Not because I want him back, but because I deserve better than this."
Her resolve hardened like steel, and she turned back toward the heart of the pack's territory.

The following morning, Selene awoke to the sounds of life stirring in the pack. Outside her small cabin, wolves shifted between their human and animal forms, preparing for the day ahead. Her limbs felt heavy from the restless night, but she forced herself to rise.

By the time she stepped outside, the pack's training ground was already buzzing with activity. Warriors sparred in pairs, their movements fluid and precise, while younger wolves practiced their transformations under the guidance of mentors.

Astrid, the pack's Beta, stood at the center of the clearing, barking orders. With her short blond hair tied back and her muscular frame, she exuded authority. Spotting Selene, Astrid raised an eyebrow.

"Decided to join the world after last night?" she asked, crossing her arms.

Selene flushed but straightened her shoulders. "I'm here to train," she said firmly.

Astrid's brow lifted higher. "You? Training?"

"Yes."

Astrid studied her for a moment, then nodded. "Fine. Grab a weapon. Let's see what you've got."

Selene walked to the weapon rack and picked up a wooden staff, its weight unfamiliar in her hands. She had never been much of a fighter—her role in the pack had always been more supportive, helping with logistics and care for the young and elderly. But she was done being the quiet, overlooked wolf.

Astrid stepped into the sparring circle, twirling a staff with practiced ease. "First rule of combat," she said, "never let your opponent know your next move."

Selene barely had time to process the words before Astrid lunged, her staff sweeping low toward Selene's legs. Instinctively, Selene jumped back, narrowly avoiding the strike.

The sparring match was brutal. Astrid held nothing back, forcing Selene to dodge, parry, and block with all her might. The other wolves began to gather, murmuring among themselves as they watched the unlikely match unfold.

Selene's movements were clumsy at first, her strikes awkward and hesitant. But with every failed attempt, she learned. She adjusted her grip, studied Astrid's movements, and began anticipating her attacks.

When Selene finally landed a strike on Astrid's shoulder, the Beta smirked. "Not bad," Astrid said, stepping back and lowering her staff. "You've got potential. But you've got a long way to go."

Selene nodded, her chest heaving. Her muscles ached, and her palms were blistered, but for the first time since the ceremony, she felt alive.

"Keep showing up," Astrid added, her voice softer now. "You've got more fight in you than you realize."

As Selene walked back toward her cabin, her head held high, she nearly collided with a tall figure stepping out of the woods.

"Sorry!" she said, looking up to see a stranger. He was broad-shouldered and lean, with sandy hair and a boyish grin that softened his sharp features. His hazel eyes sparkled with curiosity.

"No need to apologize," he said, his voice warm. "You must be Selene."

She blinked. "And you are?"

"Finn Ashford," he said, offering his hand. "I'm here from the Silverridge Pack. We're in talks with your Alpha about an alliance."

She hesitated before shaking his hand. "It's nice to meet you."

Finn's smile widened. "Likewise. I've heard a lot about you."

"About me?" she asked, surprised.

"Word travels fast," he said, shrugging. "I heard about the ceremony. About what happened."

Selene stiffened, her jaw tightening. "Then you know it's none of your business."

Finn chuckled. "Fair enough. But for what it's worth, I think Caelan's a fool."

Her eyes widened at his bluntness, but before she could respond, Finn added, "I'll see you around, Selene." With that, he turned and walked away, leaving her standing in the middle of the path, her thoughts racing.

For the first time in a long while, someone had seen her—really seen her. And as she watched Finn disappear into the trees, she couldn't help but wonder if the Moon Goddess had plans for her that went far beyond a single rejection.

CHAPTER 3: THE HUMAN INTERLOPER

The scent of coffee and freshly baked bread drifted through the pack house as Felicity Carter made her entrance. Her fiery red hair, styled to perfection, caught the morning sunlight streaming through the tall windows, and her fitted leather jacket screamed confidence. She strode in like she owned the place, her high-heeled boots clicking against the polished wooden floors, turning more than a few heads. Some of the wolves paused in their conversations, their gazes wary. Felicity wasn't one of them, and she made no effort to fit in—not that she wanted to. She thrived on standing out.

"Morning, everyone," she said breezily, flashing a dazzling smile as she reached the large communal table where Caelan sat, poring over reports with Astrid and a few other pack leaders.

Caelan barely looked up. "You're late."

"Fashionably so," she replied, draping herself into the seat next to him. "I'm not much of a morning person. You know that."

Astrid shot her a cold glance but didn't say anything, instead returning to her notes.

Felicity leaned closer to Caelan, her voice dropping. "So, what's on the agenda for today? More boring meetings? Or something a little more exciting?"

Caelan sighed, pinching the bridge of his nose. "We have training drills, territory patrols, and preparations for the Silverridge alliance. Nothing that concerns you, Felicity."

She pouted, trailing a finger along the edge of the table. "Oh, come on. I could help. Maybe spice things up around here."

"Your presence is spice enough," Astrid muttered under her breath.

Caelan shot Astrid a warning look before turning back to Felicity. "This is pack business. You don't need to get involved."

Felicity smirked. "Fine, fine. I'll leave the heavy lifting to the wolves. But you can't blame a girl for wanting to feel useful." She leaned back in her chair, her eyes sweeping over the other wolves at the table. Most of them avoided her gaze, their unease evident. She didn't care. In fact, she found their discomfort amusing.

Later that day, Felicity wandered to the training grounds, curious to see what all the fuss was about. She arrived just in time to see Selene sparring with one of the younger wolves, her movements sharp and precise.

Felicity's lips curved into a sly smile. Well, well, isn't this interesting?

Selene had changed since the rejection ceremony, and Felicity could see it. Her posture was more confident, her strikes more deliberate. There was a fire in her eyes that hadn't been there before, and it irked Felicity to no end.

"Impressive," Felicity said loudly, clapping her hands as Selene landed a clean blow on her opponent.

Selene turned, her expression guarded as she wiped sweat from her brow. "Felicity," she said coolly. "What are you doing here?"

"Just observing," Felicity said with a shrug, sauntering closer. "I didn't realize you were so... determined."

Selene narrowed her eyes. "What's that supposed to mean?"

"Oh, nothing," Felicity said, her voice dripping with mock innocence. "It's just surprising, that's all. I mean, after everything that happened with Caelan, I'd have thought you'd want to keep a low profile."

Selene bristled, but she held her ground. "I don't let setbacks define me. Unlike some people, I actually believe in earning respect."

A ripple of murmurs spread through the wolves watching nearby. Felicity's smile faltered for a moment, but she quickly recovered.

"Touché," Felicity said, her tone saccharine. "But let's not pretend, shall we? You're just trying to prove something to Caelan."

Selene stepped closer, her voice steady. "I don't need to prove anything to him. Or to you."

Felicity's eyes flashed with irritation, but she forced a laugh. "Oh, sweetie, don't take it so personally. I'm just here to make sure everyone knows where they stand. And right now, that's beneath me."

Selene stared at her for a long moment, then turned back to her sparring partner, dismissing Felicity without another word. The subtle rejection stung more than Felicity cared to admit, and as she walked away, her fists clenched at her sides.

That evening, Felicity cornered Caelan in his office, where he was reviewing the latest patrol reports.

"You need to do something about her," Felicity said, her voice sharp.

Caelan didn't look up. "About who?"

"Selene," she snapped, pacing the room. "She's stirring things up. Everyone's talking about her like she's some kind of hero. It's ridiculous."

Caelan finally set the reports aside, his brow furrowing. "She's training. That's what wolves do, Felicity. It's not your concern."

"But it is my concern," she insisted, crossing her arms. "I'm supposed to be part of your life, Caelan. How can I be when she's constantly hanging around, making me look bad?"

Caelan sighed, leaning back in his chair. "Selene isn't doing anything to you. You're the one making this an issue."

Felicity's cheeks flushed with anger. "You're defending her?"

"I'm not defending anyone," he said, his voice firm. "I'm asking you to let it go."

Felicity stared at him, her jaw tightening. She wasn't used to being brushed off, and it stung more than she cared to admit. "Fine," she said, her tone icy. "But don't say I didn't warn you when she turns the pack against you."

She stormed out, leaving Caelan alone with his thoughts.

As the door slammed behind her, he rubbed his temples, frustration bubbling under the surface. He didn't have the energy to deal with Felicity's theatrics, not when his mind kept drifting back to Selene. He had seen her on the training grounds earlier, her determination shining through every move she made.

For a moment, he allowed himself to wonder if he had made a mistake.

CHAPTER 4: SPARKS OF DEFIANCE

The chill of dawn had barely lifted when Selene arrived at the training grounds again, the soreness from the previous day settling into her muscles. She welcomed the ache—it was proof she was growing stronger, proof she wasn't the same quiet girl who had been rejected under the moonlight.
Astrid was already there, overseeing the morning drills. The Beta gave Selene a brief nod of acknowledgment, her expression unreadable.
"Back for more?" Astrid asked, her tone brisk.
Selene met her gaze steadily. "I'm not quitting. Not until I'm as strong as the rest of them."
A flicker of approval crossed Astrid's face before she gestured toward the weapons rack. "Pick your poison, then. Let's see how determined you really are."
As Selene moved to grab a practice sword, she felt a ripple of awareness sweep through the clearing. The pack was watching her. Again.
Among them was Finn. He leaned casually against a nearby tree, his hazel eyes tracking her every movement with a mixture of curiosity and admiration.
"Looks like you've got an audience," Astrid murmured, smirking.
Selene rolled her eyes but couldn't help the faint flush that crept up her neck. She ignored Finn and focused on the task at hand, stepping into the sparring circle with one of the senior warriors.
The match was intense. The warrior's strikes were calculated and powerful, forcing Selene to rely on speed and strategy rather than brute strength. Each time she blocked a blow or managed a counterstrike, her confidence grew.
When the match ended with Selene disarming her opponent in a burst of adrenaline-fueled precision, the onlookers broke into scattered applause.
Finn whistled from the sidelines. "Now that was impressive."

Selene shot him a glance, shaking her head but unable to suppress a small smile.

After training, Selene lingered by the edge of the forest, catching her breath and savoring the rare moment of peace. The sound of approaching footsteps made her turn, and she found Finn walking toward her.
"Hey," he said, his tone easy and friendly. "Mind if I join you?"
Selene shrugged. "It's a free forest."
He chuckled, falling into step beside her. For a while, they walked in silence, the soft rustle of leaves and the distant calls of birds filling the space between them.
"You've got a lot of guts," Finn said finally, his voice thoughtful.
Selene glanced at him. "What do you mean?"
"Coming out here every day, training like your life depends on it," he replied. "Most people would've folded after what you went through. But you're... different."
His words caught her off guard, and for a moment, she didn't know how to respond. "I just don't want to feel weak anymore," she said quietly.
Finn stopped, turning to face her. "You're not weak, Selene. Not by a long shot."
There was something in his gaze—earnestness, admiration—that made her chest tighten. She had spent so long feeling invisible, unworthy. Finn's words felt like a balm to wounds she hadn't even realized were still open.
"Thank you," she said softly.
He grinned. "Anytime."

Across the pack grounds, Caelan watched from his office window as Selene and Finn walked together, their easy camaraderie stirring an uncomfortable heat in his chest.
He had told himself he didn't care—that his rejection of Selene had been the right decision. But watching her now, standing taller and smiling in a way he hadn't seen before, he couldn't deny the pang of... something.
Jealousy?

No. That couldn't be it.
Felicity's voice interrupted his thoughts. "You're staring."
Caelan turned sharply to find her leaning against the doorframe, her arms crossed and a knowing smirk on her lips.
"I'm not staring," he said gruffly, turning away.
"Oh, please," Felicity said, sauntering into the room. "You've been glued to that window for the past five minutes." She glanced outside, her smirk fading when she saw who he had been watching. "Her again?"
Caelan didn't answer, which was answer enough.
Felicity's tone sharpened. "She's trying to get under your skin, you know. Parading around with that Silverridge wolf like she's some sort of prize."
"Leave it, Felicity," Caelan warned, his voice low.
But she didn't. "You rejected her, Caelan. Isn't that what you wanted? So why are you wasting your time thinking about her now?"
His jaw tightened, and he turned to face her, his expression hard. "Because this is my pack, and I make it my business to know what's going on. Don't mistake that for anything else."
Felicity's lips thinned, but she didn't press further. Instead, she gave a mocking shrug. "Fine. But don't come crying to me when she decides she's better off somewhere else."
With that, she stormed out, leaving Caelan alone with his tangled thoughts.

That evening, Selene sat outside her cabin, gazing up at the stars. The day had been long and grueling, but for the first time in a while, she felt a spark of hope. She was stronger than she had thought, more capable than anyone had given her credit for—including herself.
A soft knock at her door broke her reverie. When she opened it, she found Finn standing there, holding a bundle wrapped in cloth.
"What's this?" she asked, puzzled.
He grinned, handing it to her. "Open it and see."

Unwrapping the cloth, she found a finely crafted dagger with an intricately engraved hilt. It was beautiful and deadly, perfectly balanced in her hand.

"Finn… I can't accept this," she said, looking up at him.

"Sure you can," he said easily. "Think of it as a token of encouragement. You're going to do great things, Selene. I can feel it."

She stared at the dagger, her throat tightening with emotion. "Thank you," she said, her voice barely above a whisper.

He smiled, his hazel eyes warm. "Anytime."

As Finn walked away, Selene felt the weight of the blade in her hand and the weight of something else in her heart—a growing realization that maybe, just maybe, she wasn't as alone as she thought.

And somewhere in the shadows, Caelan watched the sight of Finn and Selene together reigniting the fire in his chest. A fire he was no longer sure he could control.

CHAPTER 5: CRACKS IN THE ALPHA'S ARMOR

The Alpha's quarters were a blend of imposing strength and understated elegance, a reflection of Caelan himself. Heavy oak furniture, rich leather accents, and a roaring fireplace gave the space an air of authority. Yet tonight, the room felt oppressive.

Caelan sat at his desk, his fingers drumming against the polished wood as he tried to focus on the alliance documents from the Silverridge pack. But no matter how hard he tried, his mind kept drifting—to the training grounds, to the sparring matches, and to the way Selene had laughed with Finn.

The faint sound of boots on the stone floor outside his door drew his attention. Moments later, Astrid entered without knocking, her no-nonsense demeanor as sharp as ever.

"You've been brooding," she stated, dropping a stack of reports onto his desk.

"I don't brood," Caelan replied, leaning back in his chair.

Astrid arched an eyebrow, clearly unconvinced. "You've been pacing your office for hours. That's what I call brooding."

Caelan let out a frustrated sigh. "Is there a reason you're here, Astrid?"

"Yes," she said, crossing her arms. "We need to finalize the Silverridge patrol routes before the next full moon. And while we're at it, we should talk about Selene."

At the mention of her name, Caelan stiffened. "What about her?"

"She's turning heads," Astrid said bluntly. "The pack's starting to notice her progress. She's not the same quiet wolf she was a few weeks ago."

"Good," Caelan said gruffly. "She's finally stepping up."

Astrid's gaze sharpened. "And that doesn't bother you? Because from where I'm standing, it seems like you've been paying a lot of attention to her lately."

Caelan's jaw clenched. "I'm paying attention to the pack. That's my job."

Astrid snorted. "Right. And the way you've been glaring at Finn every time he talks to her? That's just you doing your job, too?"

Caelan didn't answer, and the silence spoke volumes.

Astrid softened slightly, her tone losing some of its edge. "Look, Caelan, I know rejecting her was supposed to be the smart move. An Alpha choosing a human mate? It keeps things simple. But you need to ask yourself if it was the right move."

"I don't have time for this," Caelan said, standing abruptly. "The alliance needs my focus."

Astrid shook her head, a faint smirk on her lips. "You can lie to yourself all you want, but the rest of us can see it. You're jealous."

With that, she left, leaving Caelan alone with the firelight and the gnawing truth in her words.

Meanwhile, Selene was walking back to her cabin, the dagger Finn had given her tucked securely at her side. The blade felt like a symbol of something greater—a reminder of her growing strength and the new path she was carving for herself.

As she reached her door, she heard a voice behind her. "Selene."

She turned to see Caelan standing a few feet away, his expression unreadable. His presence was as commanding as ever, and despite everything, her heart gave an unbidden flutter.

"What do you want?" she asked, her tone wary.

"I wanted to check on you," he said.

Her eyes narrowed. "Why? You've made it clear I'm none of your concern."

Caelan hesitated, his gaze flickering to the dagger at her side. "You've been spending a lot of time with Finn."
Selene crossed her arms. "And that bothers you because...?"
"It doesn't," he said quickly, though his tone betrayed him. "I just want to make sure you're being careful. Silverridge wolves can be—"
"Can be what?" she interrupted, her voice sharp. "You don't get to lecture me, Caelan. Not after everything you've done."
His jaw tightened, but he didn't look away. "You're part of this pack, Selene. That means your choices affect all of us."
She took a step closer, her eyes blazing. "My choices? You mean the ones I've been forced to make because you rejected me? Because you chose her over me?"
Caelan flinched, the truth of her words hitting him like a blow. "I made the best decision for the pack," he said finally, his voice low.
"No," Selene said, her voice steady but full of conviction. "You made the easiest decision for yourself. And now, you can't stand that I'm moving on."
The air between them was thick with tension, their emotions swirling like a storm. For a moment, neither of them spoke, their gazes locked in a battle of wills.
Finally, Caelan broke the silence. "You're stronger than I gave you credit for."
Selene blinked, taken aback by the unexpected admission.
"But don't let Finn distract you from what's important," he added, his tone softening.
She let out a bitter laugh. "What's important? Like proving my worth to a pack that's never seen me? Like trying to exist under the shadow of your rejection?"
Her words struck a chord, and Caelan looked away, unable to meet her eyes.
"Goodnight, Alpha," she said, her tone icy as she turned and entered her cabin, leaving him standing alone under the moonlight.

Back in his office, Caelan paced restlessly, Astrid's words and Selene's accusations swirling in his mind. The fire crackled in the hearth, but it did little to ease the growing turmoil in his chest.

Choosing Felicity had been logical. Strategic. But logic didn't explain the way his chest tightened whenever he saw Selene smile, or the way his temper flared when Finn was near her.

He poured himself a glass of whiskey, downing it in one gulp as he stared out the window into the night.

For the first time since the ceremony, doubt crept into his mind, whispering a question he couldn't ignore:

What if I was wrong?

CHAPTER 6: THE ALPHA'S FRAYING RESOLVE

The Silverridge wolves arrived at noon, their sleek, powerful forms a sharp contrast to the rugged terrain of the Blackstone pack's forested territory. They traveled in their human forms for diplomacy's sake, but the aura of strength surrounding them was unmistakable.

Selene stood near the edge of the gathering crowd, her curiosity piqued as the visitors dismounted their dark horses and stepped forward. Finn was among them, his easy smile setting him apart from the more stoic expressions of his packmates. He spotted her immediately and gave a small wave, which she returned with a faint smile.

Not far from her, Caelan stood at the forefront of the Blackstone wolves, his stance firm and his expression unreadable. His sharp eyes took in every detail of the Silverridge delegation, though they lingered a second too long on Finn greeting Selene.

"Alpha Blackstone," the Silverridge Alpha said, his deep voice cutting through the murmurs. He was a tall man with gray streaks in his beard and a calculating gleam in his eyes. "Thank you for hosting us."

"Alpha Graythorne," Caelan replied with a nod, his tone formal. "Welcome to Blackstone. We've prepared accommodations for your pack and space for any joint training exercises you'd like to conduct."

The two Alphas shook hands, the weight of the alliance resting heavy between them.

As the day unfolded, the two packs mingled, though the interactions were laced with subtle tension. Selene found herself drawn into a conversation with Finn and a few other

Silverridge wolves, their humor and warmth a refreshing change from the cool scrutiny she often endured.

"So, you're the famous Selene we've heard about," teased one of the Silverridge females, her tone light.

Selene blinked in surprise. "Famous?"

Finn chuckled. "Word travels fast between packs. You've made quite an impression."

Selene felt a flicker of pride. It was strange to think of herself as someone worth noticing, but Finn's easy confidence in her was infectious.

As they talked, Caelan watched from a distance, his jaw tightening with every laugh that escaped Selene's lips. He told himself it was nothing, just his natural instinct as Alpha to monitor interactions between the packs. But even he couldn't deny the pang of jealousy burning in his chest.

"She seems happy," Astrid commented, appearing beside him.

Caelan didn't respond, his gaze fixed on Selene.

Astrid smirked. "You know, staring won't solve anything."

"I'm not staring," Caelan said tersely, though he didn't look away.

Astrid sighed. "You're going to have to deal with this eventually, Caelan. You can't keep pretending it doesn't bother you."

"It doesn't," he snapped.

Astrid raised an eyebrow but said nothing more, leaving him alone with his turbulent thoughts.

Later that evening, the packs gathered for a feast in the great hall. The room was alive with the hum of conversation, the clinking of glasses, and the rich aroma of roasted meats and spices.

Selene sat with Finn at one of the long tables, their laughter carrying above the din as they exchanged stories. She felt a lightness she hadn't experienced in months, a sense of belonging that had been missing since Caelan's rejection.

Caelan sat at the head of the table, Felicity by his side. She leaned into him, her hand resting possessively on his arm as

she chatted with one of the Silverridge wolves. Despite her charm, she couldn't seem to capture Caelan's full attention, his eyes continually drifting to Selene.
The sight of her with Finn, their heads close together as they laughed, made his grip tighten around his glass.
Felicity noticed.
"Everything okay, darling?" she asked sweetly, her voice cutting through his thoughts.
"I'm fine," he said shortly, setting his glass down with more force than necessary.
Felicity followed his gaze, her expression darkening when she saw Selene. "She certainly has a way of making herself the center of attention, doesn't she?"
Caelan didn't reply, but Felicity wasn't done.
"Maybe it's time someone reminded her of her place," she said, her tone dripping with malice.

After the feast, the hall began to empty as wolves retired for the night. Selene stepped outside, savoring the crisp night air. She leaned against one of the wooden posts of the porch, the stars above casting a silvery glow over the pack grounds.
"You looked like you were having fun tonight," a familiar voice said behind her.
She turned to see Caelan standing a few feet away, his hands tucked into his pockets.
"It was a good night," she replied cautiously.
He stepped closer, the shadows playing across his face. "Finn seems to like you."
Selene stiffened at his words, her defenses rising. "Why do you care?"
"I'm your Alpha," he said, his tone steady but his eyes conflicted. "It's my job to care."
"No," she said firmly, standing her ground. "You lost the right to care about me when you rejected me. Remember?"
Her words were a slap, but he didn't flinch. Instead, he took another step closer, his voice dropping. "Do you really think he's what you want?"

Selene's breath caught at the intensity in his gaze. "What I want doesn't concern you, Caelan. You made sure of that."
He reached out as if to touch her but stopped himself, his hand falling back to his side. "You deserve better than him."
She laughed bitterly. "And what, you think you're better? After what you put me through?"
The raw emotion in her voice cut through him, and for a moment, he didn't know what to say.
"I—" he began, but she shook her head.
"Save it," she said, her voice trembling with anger. "I'm done letting you control how I feel. You chose Felicity. Stick with her."
She turned and walked away, leaving him standing alone under the stars.

Inside the pack house, Felicity watched from the shadows, her fists clenched at her sides. She had seen the exchange between Caelan and Selene, and it confirmed her worst fears. Selene wasn't just a threat—she was a rival.
And Felicity wasn't about to let anyone take what was hers. As she slipped away into the darkness, a dangerous glint in her eyes, she began to plot. If Selene wanted to challenge her, she would regret it.

CHAPTER 7: SHADOWS OF DECEPTION

The morning sun crept over the forest, its golden rays filtering through the trees and casting dappled patterns on the ground. Selene awoke to the sound of soft knocking at her cabin door.

Pulling a blanket around her shoulders, she shuffled to the door and opened it to find Astrid standing there, her sharp eyes unusually soft.

"Early start today," Selene mumbled, rubbing her eyes.

Astrid smirked. "Get dressed. We're heading to the eastern border for training with the Silverridge warriors."

Selene perked up at the news. Training with the Silverridge wolves meant another chance to prove herself—and to see Finn. She nodded quickly, shutting the door to prepare.

By the time she joined the group heading out, the air was buzzing with energy. Finn greeted her with a broad smile, while Caelan observed the gathering from a distance, his expression as unreadable as ever.

The eastern border was a stretch of rugged terrain, with rocky outcroppings and dense underbrush that made it a perfect training ground. Wolves from both packs paired off for sparring matches and agility drills, their movements a blur of speed and power.

Selene found herself paired with Finn for sparring. As they squared off, she couldn't help but notice the way his smile softened the sharp angles of his face.

"Ready to lose?" he teased, twirling a wooden practice sword in his hand.

She smirked. "Not a chance."

Their match was fast-paced, filled with laughter and banter that belied the intensity of their strikes. Selene's movements were quicker than ever, her growing confidence evident with each swing of her blade.

"You're getting too good at this," Finn said as he dodged a particularly close strike.

"Maybe you're just slowing down," she shot back, grinning.

Nearby, Caelan watched the exchange, his jaw clenched tight. He tried to focus on the training of his own pack members, but his eyes kept straying back to Selene. The way she laughed with Finn, the easy camaraderie between them—it was like a thorn in his side.

Astrid, standing beside him, noticed his distraction and leaned in. "If you grip your sword any tighter, it's going to snap."

Caelan shot her a warning glance, but she only smirked in response.

As the training session wound down, the group gathered to rest and share water. Selene sat with Finn beneath a tree, their conversation flowing effortlessly.

"I don't think I've ever seen you smile this much," Finn said, his tone teasing but warm.

Selene shrugged, her cheeks tinged with color. "I guess I've just... found my footing."

"You're stronger than most people give you credit for," he said, his gaze serious now. "Don't ever forget that."

Her chest tightened at his words, a mix of gratitude and something deeper swelling within her.

But before she could respond, Felicity appeared, her presence like a sudden chill.

"Selene," Felicity said sweetly, though her tone held an edge. "Can I borrow you for a moment?"

Selene frowned, hesitant to leave the comfort of Finn's company, but she nodded. "Of course."

Felicity led her a short distance away, her expression shifting the moment they were out of earshot.

"You've been awfully cozy with Finn," Felicity said, her tone sharp now.

Selene crossed her arms, refusing to back down. "Why does that matter to you?"

Felicity's eyes narrowed. "It matters because you're making a spectacle of yourself. You might think you're earning respect, but all you're doing is embarrassing the pack."

Selene's jaw tightened. "I don't need your approval, Felicity."

Felicity stepped closer, her voice dropping to a venomous whisper. "You're a distraction, Selene. To Finn. To Caelan. To everyone. Maybe you should think about stepping back before you cause any more trouble."

Selene stared at her, anger bubbling beneath the surface. "If you have a problem with me, Felicity, just say it. Don't dance around it."

"Oh, I'll say it," Felicity said, her smile cruel. "Stay away from Finn. Stay away from Caelan. Stay in your lane, and maybe you won't ruin what little place you have here."

Without waiting for a response, Felicity turned and walked away, leaving Selene fuming.

That night, Selene sat outside her cabin, her mind racing with Felicity's words. The frustration she had felt earlier boiled over, a knot of anger and hurt twisting in her chest.

She gripped the dagger Finn had given her, its cool weight a small comfort in the chaos of her emotions. She had come so far, fought so hard to prove herself, and yet Felicity still treated her like she was nothing.

The sound of footsteps made her look up. Finn was approaching, his expression concerned.

"Are you okay?" he asked, sitting beside her on the steps.

Selene hesitated, then nodded. "Just... a lot on my mind."

Finn studied her for a moment before speaking. "Did Felicity say something to you?"

Selene's silence was answer enough.

"She doesn't speak for the pack," Finn said firmly. "And she doesn't speak for me. You're stronger than she'll ever admit, Selene. Don't let her get to you."

His words warmed her, and she managed a small smile. "Thank you, Finn."

As they sat together under the stars, a sense of calm settled over Selene. For the first time in a long while, she felt like she wasn't alone.

Across the pack grounds, Caelan stood on the balcony of his quarters, his gaze fixed on the two figures sitting together. Felicity entered the room behind him, her arms crossed.
"You're letting this go on?"
Caelan didn't respond, his expression shadowed.
"She's making a fool of you," Felicity said sharply. "Flirting with Finn like that, parading herself around as if she's important."
"Enough, Felicity," Caelan said, his voice low but firm.
Felicity's eyes widened, stunned by his tone. "You're defending her now?"
"I'm saying leave it," he replied, turning to face her. "Focus on your own role here. Selene is none of your concern."
Felicity's mouth tightened into a thin line, fury flashing in her eyes. "If you don't handle her, I will," she hissed before storming out.
Caelan watched her go, his chest tight with frustration. His mind replayed Selene's laughter, the determination in her eyes during training, the spark that had drawn him to her from the start.
Felicity's words echoed in his mind, but they couldn't drown out the truth he had been avoiding.
Selene wasn't just a member of his pack.
She was the one he had pushed away—and the one he couldn't stop thinking about.

CHAPTER 8: TENSIONS UNLEASHED

The next few days in the Blackstone pack were marked by an undercurrent of tension. The Silverridge wolves had stayed longer than expected, and the joint training sessions had intensified. While Selene continued to prove herself—her agility and fierce determination earning nods of approval from both packs—Caelan's brooding presence was impossible to ignore. He kept his distance, his focus on pack matters, but it was clear to everyone that his gaze often lingered on Selene, especially when she was in the company of Finn.

Selene, for her part, did her best to stay focused. She didn't have time for the complicated emotions Caelan stirred up within her anymore. She had spent so many years under his shadow, longing for something he had refused to give her. Now, she was finally gaining the respect she deserved, and she couldn't afford to let him distract her.

It was late afternoon when Selene and Finn found themselves once again at the eastern border, sharpening their skills. The day had been hot, and the air felt thick with the impending storm that had been building all afternoon. She could feel it, an electrical charge in the air—like the world was on the verge of snapping.

"Let's take a break," Finn suggested, wiping the sweat from his brow.

Selene nodded gratefully, stepping back from the sparring ring. She noticed a few wolves from Silverridge watching, but her attention was drawn to a figure standing just beyond the circle. Caelan. His dark eyes tracked her movements with an intensity that made her stomach twist.

Her pulse quickened, but she forced herself to look away. She didn't need this. She didn't need him.

"Selene."

She turned, surprised to find Finn standing next to her. His expression was soft, genuine. "I know what you're thinking," he said quietly, his voice steady. "But don't let him get to you. You're stronger than this."

Her chest tightened. It was the same thing Finn had said before. She didn't need to hear it anymore. She wanted to move on, to carve out a space for herself where she wasn't constantly battling between the past and the present.

"I'm fine, Finn," she said, forcing a smile. "Really."

Finn studied her, his eyes narrowing slightly. "Okay. But don't think I'm not paying attention. You deserve to be happy, Selene. Don't let him or anyone else hold you back."

Before she could respond, the sound of footsteps reached their ears, followed by a voice that sent a chill down her spine.

"Selene."

It was Caelan.

She tensed, her gaze flicking to Finn, then to Caelan. His jaw was tight, his posture rigid. He looked every bit the Alpha he was, but there was something else there—something she couldn't quite place.

"Alpha," she said, her tone cool.

Caelan's eyes flickered briefly to Finn before returning to her. "I need to speak with you."

Finn stepped forward, his body stiffening. "Is there a problem?"

Caelan's gaze hardened. "I don't believe it's any of your concern, Finn."

Selene's chest tightened at the subtle threat in Caelan's voice, but she quickly stepped in between them, her hand raising slightly. "It's fine, Finn," she said, her voice firm. "I'll handle this."

Finn shot her one last look, clearly displeased, but he nodded and walked away, giving her the space she needed.

When he was out of earshot, Selene turned to Caelan, her irritation bubbling to the surface. "What do you want, Caelan? To lecture me again?"

His expression softened for a moment, but his eyes still burned with an intensity that unsettled her. "No. I just need to talk to you. Alone."

Selene crossed her arms, eyes narrowing. "Fine. What's so urgent?"

Caelan hesitated, glancing over his shoulder to make sure no one was watching. When he spoke, his voice was low, almost hesitant. "You're pushing everyone away, Selene."

The words stung more than she cared to admit, and she swallowed hard before speaking. "I'm not pushing anyone away. I'm just finally living for myself. Something I've never been able to do until now."

Caelan's eyes darkened, but there was a flicker of something else in them—guilt? Regret?

"You're shutting people out," he pressed, his voice softer now, like he was trying to break through some invisible barrier she had erected between them. "Finn's trying to get close to you, and you're just brushing him off. He cares about you, you know."

Selene's breath hitched, but she masked it with a sharp laugh. "He cares about me? Or is it just that he sees me as some challenge he needs to conquer?"

"Don't twist it," Caelan said, frustration creeping into his voice. "You know that's not what I meant."

Her chest tightened as her emotions swirled. She didn't want to listen to him. Didn't want to care. But his presence—so close, so undeniable—made her want to rip away the walls she'd spent years building.

"What do you want from me, Caelan?" she demanded. "You rejected me. You chose Felicity. What do you expect me to do now? Forget all of that? Act like it doesn't matter?"

His jaw clenched as he took a step toward her, his voice almost a whisper. "I never wanted to hurt you, Selene. You have to know that."

But the words were hollow. She had heard them before, years ago, and they had done nothing to heal the wounds he had caused.

"I don't need your apologies," she said, her voice trembling with restrained emotion. "I need you to stay out of my way. I'm done being the girl you can't decide what to do with."

Caelan flinched at her words, but before he could reply, a distant howl echoed across the land—a sharp, chilling sound that broke through the tension like a crack of thunder.
The moment was shattered.
Caelan's posture stiffened, and Selene's heart skipped a beat. This was no ordinary howl. It was urgent, laced with panic and pain.
Without another word, Caelan spun on his heel, his body already shifting into wolf form as he sprinted towards the sound.
Selene didn't hesitate. She followed suit, shifting into her own wolf form and loping after him, her instincts taking over.

When they reached the western perimeter, they found the source of the howl—a lone wolf from Silverridge, bloodied and barely conscious. He was slumped against a tree, his fur matted with dirt and blood.
"Get him to the healer," Caelan barked at his pack, his voice cold and commanding.
Selene stepped forward, her heart pounding as she knelt beside the injured wolf. "What happened?" she asked, her voice steady despite the panic creeping at the edges of her mind.
"The border... was breached," the wolf gasped, his eyes clouded with pain. "A rogue pack... they're attacking... our territory."
The words hit like a punch to the gut. A rogue pack. They were the last thing the Blackstone and Silverridge wolves needed right now.
"Rogue wolves?" Selene whispered. "How many?"
"Too many," the wolf muttered. "They're already pushing through. Alpha Graythorne knows we're vulnerable... they've planned this for weeks."
Caelan's eyes met hers, dark and filled with something she couldn't quite read. "We have to move. Now."
Selene didn't need any more urging. She sprinted into the woods, the weight of the situation sinking in. She had no idea what awaited them, but one thing was clear—this was no

longer about past grudges or unresolved feelings. This was about survival.
And it was going to take everything they had to defend what they'd built.

As Caelan and Selene raced through the trees, there was no time for anything but the fight ahead. But in the back of both their minds, the unspoken truth lingered—things were about to change.

CHAPTER 9: THE FIRST STRIKE

The night had fallen heavy, with the scent of impending rain in the air, and the wind carried a chill that whispered through the trees. The forest was alive with the sound of rustling leaves and the distant calls of wolves from both packs—an eerie tension in the air. Selene's heart beat in time with the rhythm of her paws as she ran, her body instinctively following Caelan's lead through the forest.
They had only just received the news of the rogue pack's arrival, but every second felt like an eternity. They were outnumbered, and time was quickly running out. She didn't know much about the rogue pack, only that their Alpha, Graythorne, had a reputation for being ruthless, a wolf who would stop at nothing to take what he wanted.
The Silverridge wolves were already mobilizing. Caelan had given the orders to meet at the border, but he hadn't said what the plan was yet, and Selene's mind raced with possibilities. It wasn't just about protecting territory anymore—it was about protecting the pack and the people she had come to care about.
Her paws dug into the earth as she ran, her breath coming in quick, controlled bursts. She was fast—one of the fastest wolves in the pack—but the anxiety clawing at her chest made her feel like she was running through molasses. She had to focus. She couldn't let fear take over.

When they reached the clearing near the border, Selene skidded to a stop. The scene was chaos. Several of the Silverridge wolves were already in wolf form, forming a defensive line, their eyes flicking between the forest and the shadows of the trees. There was a crackling tension in the air, and even the wind had gone still.
Caelan's sharp voice cut through the silence, commanding his pack with the calm authority of an Alpha. "Spread out. Watch

for any signs of movement. Keep your eyes open. We're dealing with a well-coordinated attack."

Selene shifted back into her human form, the tension in her shoulders coiling tighter with each passing second. She wasn't just a warrior—she was an integral part of this pack now, and this attack was testing everything she had learned over the past few months. As much as she wanted to impress Caelan, she knew this wasn't the time for personal battles. The lives of her pack members were on the line.

Finn arrived seconds later, panting from the run but looking determined. His eyes locked with Selene's, and there was a moment—a brief, silent exchange—where she saw something in his gaze that wasn't there before. It was the same way he had looked at her earlier that day, the unspoken words between them thicker than the air around them.

"Ready?" Finn asked, his voice low but filled with purpose. His muscles were taut, his body primed for action.

"As ready as I'll ever be," Selene answered, trying to ignore the nerves that made her stomach flutter.

Caelan was standing in the center of the clearing now, his posture firm and regal. His eyes were dark with determination as he scanned the forest's edge. He turned to his second-in-command, Astrid, who was already in her wolf form, muscles rippling under her fur as she waited for orders.

"Astrid, take a small group and circle the perimeter. We need to know where they're coming from. Don't engage unless you have no choice."

Astrid nodded, her amber eyes gleaming as she darted off into the woods, disappearing into the darkness like a shadow.

Caelan's gaze shifted back to Selene. He didn't speak, but his eyes held something—something deeper than leadership. It was a look she didn't quite understand, but it made her heart race.

The minutes stretched into hours, and the wait was unbearable. The night grew darker still, and every rustle of leaves, every snap of a twig made Selene's muscles tense in anticipation. She stood next to Finn, the weight of her sword heavy at her side. The air felt thick—pregnant with the expectation of something terrible.

Suddenly, the silence was shattered by a loud crack, a tree breaking in the distance. Selene's heart skipped a beat. Caelan's voice rang out, clear and commanding. "Position yourselves! They're coming!"

The forest came alive as wolves shifted back into their animal forms, the sound of growling and snarling filling the air as they took their positions. Selene's instincts kicked in, her eyes scanning the forest for any signs of movement.

And then they came—shadowy figures moving swiftly through the trees, their red eyes gleaming with malice.

"Rogues," Finn muttered, his voice tight with anger.

Selene's breath hitched. They were here.

In the blink of an eye, the first rogue lunged. A massive, dark wolf with fur as black as coal. It collided with one of the Silverridge wolves, throwing him to the ground. The sound of the impact was deafening, followed by the sounds of growls and snarls as the battle erupted.

Selene shifted quickly, leaping into action. She met the first rogue with a powerful swipe of her claws, the force sending him stumbling back. She could feel the rush of adrenaline surge through her veins as she faced off against him, her heart racing.

The rogue snarled and lunged again, but Selene was ready. She ducked beneath his attack, her claws slashing through the air to catch him across the side. He howled in pain, but before she could land another blow, a second rogue appeared, coming at her from the side.

Finn was there in an instant, his wolf form fast and precise, tackling the rogue to the ground with a vicious snarl. The two wolves fought, their teeth flashing in the dim light of the forest.

"Watch your back!" Selene shouted, barely dodging another rogue's attack.

But the chaos of the fight made everything a blur. Wolves clashed, fur flying in every direction, the ground slick with blood and dirt. The smell of the battle filled her nose, but she focused on her opponent—the rogue who had been relentless in his pursuit.

As she prepared for another strike, a voice called out from the distance.

"Caelan!"

It was Astrid. Selene's heart skipped a beat as the Silverridge second-in-command's voice echoed through the clearing.

"Graythorne is here!" Astrid shouted, her voice frantic. "He's leading the charge! We need to fall back!"

Graythorne. The rogue Alpha. Selene's blood ran cold at the mention of his name. If he was here, things were worse than they'd imagined.

Without hesitation, Caelan issued the command. "Retreat! Get back to the main camp. Defend the perimeter!"

But as Selene turned to follow the retreat, a massive force slammed into her from behind, sending her crashing to the ground. Her vision swam as she struggled to regain her bearings, but a low growl rumbled in her ears.

She twisted, only to find herself face to face with a massive, terrifying wolf—gray fur streaked with dark patches of blood. The rogue Alpha, Graythorne himself.

"I've been waiting for this," Graythorne growled, his voice guttural. "You've made this easy, little wolf."

Selene's heart pounded in her chest. This wasn't just an attack—it was a warning. Graythorne wasn't here to conquer territory. He was here to break them.

In the distance, Caelan's roar of fury filled the air. "Selene!"

But Selene's world had narrowed to the rogue Alpha standing before her, the sound of her own breath mingling with his growl. She wasn't sure if it was the adrenaline or the fear, but something inside her snapped.

No more running. No more hiding.

She lunged at Graythorne, her claws outstretched, teeth bared.

The battle was far from over. But for the first time, Selene knew something deep within her—this fight was hers to win.

CHAPTER 10: THE PRICE OF VICTORY

The moment Selene's claws struck the rogue Alpha's thick fur, a rush of adrenaline surged through her veins. She could feel the power in her muscles, the raw energy she had honed over the years. But Graythorne was no ordinary rogue. His strength was formidable, his eyes gleaming with a savage hunger. He didn't flinch at her attack—instead, he grinned, his fangs bared like a predator toying with its prey.
"You think you can stop me, little wolf?" he sneered, his deep voice like gravel scraping across stone.
Before Selene could react, Graythorne lunged at her with terrifying speed, his powerful jaws snapping just inches from her throat. She barely had time to roll away, her body twisting in midair as she landed in a crouch. Her heart pounded, and she could feel the blood racing in her veins, the weight of the fight pressing down on her like a storm.
"You're not so different from the rest," Graythorne taunted, his eyes narrowing. "You hide behind the pack, behind the Alpha. You've always been weak, Selene. Always hiding behind your past."
Selene's snarl echoed through the trees, and she bared her teeth. "I'm not weak," she growled, her body tensing as she prepared to strike again. "And I'm not hiding anymore."
She darted forward, her claws flashing through the air. Graythorne swiped back with a brutal force, his claws striking against hers. The impact sent a shock of pain through her arm, but she refused to give ground. She wasn't backing down. Not this time.
"Fool," Graythorne snarled, shifting his weight and slamming into her with the full force of his body. She was knocked back, crashing into the hard ground, the air knocked from her lungs in a violent gasp. Pain lanced through her side, but she fought through it, rolling away and getting back on her feet.
The rogue Alpha advanced, circling her with deliberate malice. His grin was savage, almost gleeful. "You'll be nothing

but another notch on my belt, Selene. I'll rip you apart just like I've done to all the others."

Selene's muscles burned with exhaustion, her every breath a sharp reminder of the battle's intensity. But she was stronger than this. She had to be. This wasn't just for herself—it was for the pack, for the future they were fighting to protect.

A flash of movement caught her eye. Caelan.

The Blackstone Alpha was in the middle of a furious fight of his own, his wolf form a blur of speed and strength as he tore through the rogues. But despite the chaos, his gaze locked with Selene's. For a split second, it was as though the world slowed. His eyes softened, filled with something that caught her breath—something she couldn't name. But in that fleeting moment, she knew what was at stake. Not just the pack, but everything they had both struggled to overcome.

And then Graythorne's laugh cut through the moment, harsh and cruel. "So, the great Alpha watches as his pack falls. He's too weak to save you, Selene. You'll be mine, just like the rest."

His words were venom, designed to cut deep. Selene gritted her teeth, forcing herself to ignore the fear creeping into her mind. She couldn't let him win. Not now. Not when she'd come this far.

With a howl of defiance, she leapt at Graythorne, her body propelled by the fury of her resolve. This time, her attack was quick, deliberate. She targeted his throat, aiming for the soft spot beneath his thick fur. Her claws raked across his chest, leaving deep, bleeding gashes, but he managed to deflect the worst of the blow.

The rogue Alpha snarled in rage, his eyes flashing with pure fury. "You'll regret this, girl."

Selene gritted her teeth, pushing through the pain in her side. She couldn't stop now. She couldn't let him win.

With a final, desperate push, she launched herself at Graythorne once more. This time, her claws found their mark. Her teeth sank into his shoulder, and the rogue Alpha howled in pain. But Selene didn't let go. She dug in deeper, her body shaking with the effort.

The rogue's strength was waning, and in that moment, Caelan's voice rang out across the battlefield, sharp and commanding.
"Selene, now!"
She didn't need any further encouragement. Using every last ounce of her strength, Selene drove her claws into Graythorne's chest, piercing the heart with a final, powerful strike.
Graythorne's howl echoed through the clearing, raw and tortured. His body bucked beneath her, but Selene held firm, her fangs still buried in his flesh until the last breath left his body.
The fight around her seemed to pause as the rogue Alpha's lifeless body slumped to the ground. The clearing went still, save for the heavy panting of the wolves who had been locked in battle.
"Selene!"
Caelan's voice brought her back to reality, and she turned to see him sprinting toward her, his wolf form majestic and terrifying in its power. He was covered in blood, his fur matted, but his eyes never left her.
She pulled away from the fallen rogue, breathing heavily, her body aching from the brutal fight. She was covered in blood—some her own, some Graythorne's—but she didn't care. She had done it. She had brought him down.
Caelan's wolf slowed to a trot as he approached, his eyes scanning her for injuries. When he finally reached her, he shifted back into his human form with a growl of frustration.
"You're hurt," he said, his voice low and rough, but there was something else in his eyes—something softer, almost like relief.
"I'm fine," Selene said, her voice strained. She didn't have the strength to argue, so she let him help her steady herself. Her legs were shaky, and her side still throbbed with pain, but the adrenaline was starting to wear off, leaving her with the heavy weight of exhaustion.
Behind them, the rest of the pack had begun to regroup. The rogue wolves were retreating, their numbers significantly

reduced, but the damage was done. The ground was littered with fallen bodies, both from Blackstone and Silverridge. It had been a hard fight, but they had won.

"Good job," Caelan said, his eyes searching her face, his hand lingering on her arm. There was a hesitation in his touch, as though he was unsure of what to say, unsure of what to do. Selene met his gaze, her breath still heavy in her chest. For a moment, they just stood there, the chaos of the battlefield surrounding them. And then, without warning, a wave of exhaustion crashed over her, and she slumped against Caelan, unable to hold herself up any longer.

He caught her easily, his arms wrapping around her to steady her. His touch was warm, grounding, and for a moment, everything else faded into the background.

"You're not fine," Caelan murmured, his voice soft but laced with concern. "Let me help you."

"I don't need your help," Selene replied automatically, but the words lacked the conviction they once had. The truth was, she was exhausted—physically and emotionally. The weight of everything they had just been through was settling heavily on her shoulders, and all she wanted in that moment was to rest. To stop pretending she had it all under control.

But Caelan didn't let go. His hands were firm on her shoulders, his eyes still searching hers. "You did more than enough tonight," he said quietly. "You fought like an Alpha. But I'm not going to leave you alone."

Selene's breath caught in her throat. His words sent a ripple of emotion through her—something she couldn't quite define. She had always been strong. Always. But tonight, in this moment, she didn't have to carry the weight alone.

And for the first time, she allowed herself to lean into Caelan's strength, allowing his presence to steady her, even if just for a moment.

The fight was over, but the battle for their future—one that neither of them had fully understood until now—was just beginning.

CHAPTER 11: THE AFTERMATH

The air was heavy with the scent of blood, both wolf and human. The forest, once alive with the cacophony of howls and growls, had gone eerily quiet. The rogue pack had retreated, their Alpha, Graythorne, dead, but the cost had been steep. The Silverridge wolves had fought valiantly, but many of them bore the marks of the battle—deep gashes, bruises, and fatigue that would take days to heal.
Selene sat on a fallen log at the edge of the clearing, her body still trembling from the fight. The adrenaline that had kept her going had finally begun to ebb, leaving a raw, aching exhaustion in its wake. Her side throbbed, a constant reminder of the rogue Alpha's final strike, but it wasn't the physical pain that was weighing heavily on her heart.
It was the aftermath. The silence. The heavy burden of everything that had just happened.
"Are you sure you're alright?"
Caelan's voice cut through the silence like a soft breeze. He had returned from helping the other injured pack members, his clothes torn and stained with the blood of the battle. His eyes were darker now, haunted, and as he knelt beside her, his presence seemed to fill the space between them.
Selene nodded, forcing a smile. "I'm fine. Just... tired."
"You don't look fine." His voice was rough, filled with something unspoken. His hand hovered near her side, the touch so close she could feel the heat radiating off of him, but he didn't dare make contact.
Selene pulled her gaze away from him, looking out over the clearing instead. "I'll heal. It's nothing."
Caelan didn't respond right away. He just watched her, his gaze intense, as if he were trying to read her, to understand something she hadn't said. She felt the weight of his stare, and it made her heart beat faster. It had always been like this with him—an unspoken tension, a connection she couldn't fully explain. Not now. Not when everything was so chaotic.

"I'm not talking about your wounds," Caelan finally said, his voice low, almost too soft. "I'm talking about the weight you're carrying."

Selene stiffened, feeling a sudden lump rise in her throat. She didn't want to talk about it—not now, not when the memory of the fight still felt too fresh. But Caelan wasn't the kind of Alpha who would let her close herself off. He could see through the walls she'd built, even when she tried to keep them up.

"I'm fine, Caelan," she said again, her voice tight, defensive.

His expression darkened, his jaw tightening. "No, you're not. You're a warrior, Selene. But you're not invincible. None of us are. You can't carry everything on your own."

She turned to face him, her frustration bubbling to the surface. "I didn't ask for this. I didn't ask to be thrown into the middle of this war. But here I am. I've made my choices. I have to live with them."

Caelan's gaze softened, but there was something else in it—something that flickered beneath the surface, something she hadn't seen before. It was raw, almost vulnerable.

"You didn't choose to fight this battle. But you're still here. You chose to stand with us. And that means something."

Selene opened her mouth to respond, but the words caught in her throat. She didn't know how to explain it—how to explain the gnawing sense of responsibility that had settled into her chest ever since that first night, when she had crossed paths with Caelan. She had chosen this path, yes, but now that she was on it, it felt like there was no turning back.

"You've changed," Caelan said, his voice low but unwavering. "You're not the same wolf I met all those months ago."

Selene's heart skipped a beat at his words. The truth was, she had changed. The woman she had been before—broken, lost—felt like a distant memory now. But in some ways, she didn't recognize the person she had become either. She was no longer the lone wolf, the outsider. She was part of something bigger. She was part of this pack, and more than that—she was connected to Caelan in a way she wasn't sure she was ready to understand.

She couldn't meet his eyes. "People change."
"Yes. They do." He paused, and there was a beat of silence between them. When he spoke again, his voice was softer, almost hesitant. "But you're not alone anymore, Selene. You don't have to carry this weight by yourself."
She didn't know what to say to that. The truth was, she didn't know how to let others in. She wasn't used to leaning on anyone. She was used to standing alone, trusting only herself. But now, as Caelan knelt beside her, his presence so steady, so sure, she felt something in her begin to shift.
For the first time in a long time, Selene considered the possibility that maybe... just maybe, she didn't have to fight this battle alone.
A movement in the distance caught her attention, and she stood quickly, shaking off the quiet moment. "We should check on the others."
Caelan's hand shot out, catching her wrist before she could turn. His grip wasn't tight, but it was firm enough to stop her. "Selene." His voice was gentle but insistent. "I'm not letting you walk away from this."
She faced him again, her chest tight. She couldn't breathe. There was something in his eyes—something she hadn't been prepared for. It was a look that made her heart pound, made her blood run hot.
"I'm not walking away," she replied, though her voice was barely a whisper. "I'm here. I'm always here."
Caelan held her gaze for a long moment, as though he were trying to decide whether to say something more. His thumb brushed lightly across the back of her hand before he finally let go, a heavy sigh escaping his chest.
"Alright," he said quietly. "But don't forget what I said. We're in this together, Selene."
She nodded, swallowing hard. "Together."
With a final, lingering glance, Caelan stood and moved toward the center of the clearing, where Astrid and the others were already gathering the wounded. Selene watched him for a moment before turning her attention to the pack.

There was still so much to do. The battle wasn't truly over. Graythorne may have fallen, but the rogue threat wasn't gone —not yet. And as much as she wanted to hold onto the fragile peace in this moment, the reality of the war ahead weighed heavily on her shoulders.

The next few hours passed in a blur of activity. The Silverridge pack worked tirelessly to tend to the wounded, pulling together their resources and patching up those who had been injured during the fight. Selene did her part, checking on the injured and ensuring that the camp was secure. Her side still ached, and every movement felt like a strain, but she pushed through the pain.

Caelan stayed close, his presence constant, but there was something different in the air. The unspoken tension between them had shifted, and Selene wasn't sure if it was for better or worse. She didn't know how to reconcile the Alpha's pull with the walls she had so carefully constructed around her heart.

As night fell, the camp grew quiet, the howls of the victorious wolves echoing softly in the distance. Selene finally found a quiet spot near the edge of the camp, her body sore and exhausted, her mind racing with everything that had happened.

But as the weight of the day pressed down on her, she finally allowed herself to close her eyes. For the first time in what felt like forever, Selene felt something she hadn't felt in so long: peace.

And in the quiet of the night, with the stars watching above, Selene finally allowed herself to believe in something she had never dared to before.

Maybe, just maybe, she could belong here.

CHAPTER 12: THE CHOICE

The morning light crept through the trees, casting soft, golden beams over the clearing where the Silverridge pack had gathered. The air was still heavy with the scent of blood and sweat, the remnants of the previous night's battle hanging in the air like a lingering fog. The warriors who had fought were scattered, tending to wounds, mending armor, and making preparations for the journey back to their stronghold.

Selene stood near the edge of the clearing, her arms crossed as she watched them work. The bruising on her side had faded somewhat, but the emotional toll of the battle—of Graythorne's death, of the choices she'd made—still weighed on her. It wasn't the physical wounds that haunted her, it was the uncertainty about what came next.

"What now?"

She didn't have to turn around to know who it was. The voice was low, familiar, and carried an undercurrent of something unspoken. Caelan.

She felt his presence before she saw him—felt the warmth of his body, the weight of his eyes on her. She resisted the urge to glance over her shoulder, instead focusing on the pack members moving in the distance. They were preparing for the next phase: returning home, regrouping, making sure the rogues wouldn't have the chance to retaliate.

Caelan came to stand beside her, his posture relaxed but his eyes focused on her, studying her with an intensity that made her stomach tighten.

"You're thinking too much," he said softly.

Selene bit her lip, exhaling sharply. "I can't help it," she muttered. "There's so much to do. So many decisions to make. And I still don't know what's next for us."

For a moment, Caelan said nothing. He simply stood beside her, his presence filling the space between them. She could feel the tension in the air, but it wasn't the kind of tension that made her uneasy. It was something else—something deeper. Finally, Caelan spoke, his voice steady, his eyes searching hers. "You're not alone in this, Selene."

She let out a quiet breath. "I know."

He turned his body slightly, leaning in just enough to catch her attention. His eyes softened, almost as though he were debating something important. "You don't have to carry the weight of this all by yourself. Not anymore. I want you to know that."

Selene didn't respond immediately. Her gaze dropped to the ground, trying to collect her thoughts. It wasn't just the battle that weighed heavily on her. It was everything that had happened—the connection with Caelan, the role she had taken in the pack, and the complicated emotions that had begun to form between them. Emotions she didn't know how to handle.

"We've already lost so much, Caelan," she said quietly. "And now I'm supposed to choose between... between what's right for me and what's right for the pack. I can't do it. I can't make that choice."

Caelan's gaze sharpened. "You're not choosing between the pack and yourself. You're choosing what you want, Selene. And you deserve that. You've earned it."

Selene turned her head, finally meeting his eyes. She could see the sincerity in his expression, the weight of his words. But a part of her still couldn't let go of the fear that gripped her heart—the fear that, in choosing what she wanted, she might lose everything else.

"Then what do I do, Caelan?" she whispered, her voice trembling. "What if I make the wrong choice?"

Caelan stepped closer, his presence warm and reassuring. His hand reached out, gently resting on her shoulder, grounding her. "I'm not asking you to choose me, Selene," he said softly. "I'm asking you to choose what's best for you. The rest will follow."

The words settled around her, heavy and comforting. He wasn't pushing her. He wasn't demanding anything of her. He was simply offering her a space to breathe, to make her decision without pressure.

But there was still so much to untangle, so much to consider. "I don't know if I can," Selene confessed. "I've spent so long fighting, so long focusing on the pack. I don't even know who I am when I'm not fighting."

Caelan's expression softened even further. "You're more than just a warrior, Selene. You've been through so much. And you've come out of it stronger. But now you get to decide what comes next. You get to choose who you are—without the burden of what's already been."

Selene looked down at her hands, fingers curling into fists. She had spent so long being the soldier, the protector. But now, faced with the possibility of something more, something outside of the battle, she didn't know how to move forward.

"I don't know if I'm strong enough to make the right choice," she murmured.

"You are," Caelan replied, his voice certain. "You've always been strong enough."

There was a moment of silence between them, a stretch of time where Selene felt the weight of his words settle in her chest. She could feel his support, his belief in her. And though it didn't erase her doubts, it gave her a moment of clarity. She wasn't alone in this. She had a choice.

Her thoughts were interrupted by the distant sound of footsteps. She turned her head to see Astrid walking toward them, her face grim, her steps purposeful.

"We need to talk," Astrid said, her voice clipped.

Selene frowned, a knot forming in her stomach. "What's happened?"

Astrid stopped a few paces away, her gaze flickering between Selene and Caelan. "It's about the rogues," she said, her tone lower. "There's something we didn't account for."

"What do you mean?" Caelan asked, his voice hardening.

Astrid hesitated for a moment before speaking. "It's not just Graythorne. There's a larger force moving toward Silverridge. The rogues we fought last night were just a small part of a bigger plan. They were meant to weaken us. Now, they've set their sights on our home."

A cold chill ran down Selene's spine. "What are you saying?"

"I'm saying that the battle we fought yesterday was only the beginning," Astrid replied, her voice tight with urgency. "The rogues have a stronger pack gathering. They're coming for us. And we need to be ready."

Caelan's jaw clenched as he absorbed the information. "How soon?"

Astrid's eyes darkened. "Soon. Too soon. We need to move quickly. If we don't act fast, Silverridge will be vulnerable."

Selene felt her heart drop. She had barely come to terms with the aftermath of the battle, and now they were facing another war. The weight of responsibility settled over her once more.

"What's our plan?" Caelan asked, his voice steady despite the urgency of the situation.

Astrid looked at Selene, then at Caelan. "We'll need every wolf we can spare. And we need to rally the other packs. It's the only way we'll have a chance against the rogue force coming for us."

Selene nodded, her mind already racing with the logistics of what needed to be done. There was no time to waste.

Caelan turned to her, his eyes meeting hers. "We'll figure this out, Selene. Together."

Selene took a deep breath, her resolve hardening once more. The battle ahead would be tough, and the decisions she had to make wouldn't get any easier. But she wasn't alone. She had the pack. She had Caelan.

And for the first time, she felt ready to face whatever came next.

Later that evening, as the last of the wounded were tended to and the plans for the next phase of the war were set in motion, Selene found herself standing outside the camp. The forest around her was quiet, save for the rustling of leaves in the wind. She let the cool night air fill her lungs, trying to steady her thoughts.

A soft voice broke the silence behind her. "You're still thinking too much."

Selene turned to see Caelan approaching, his eyes soft with concern but also determination. He stopped just a few feet away from her, his presence filling the space between them like a warm beacon in the night.

"Maybe," she said with a quiet smile. "But I'm starting to think that's just who I am."

Caelan's lips curved upward, but there was an intensity in his gaze that made her pulse quicken.

"You don't have to be that way with me," he said, his voice low. "You don't have to carry everything by yourself. Not anymore."

Selene's heart skipped a beat. She had spent so long trying to carry the weight of everything alone. But in Caelan's gaze, she saw something different—something she hadn't expected.

She wasn't alone anymore.

"I know," she whispered. "I just don't know how to stop."

Caelan took a step closer, his eyes never leaving hers. "Let me help you."

And for the first time in a long time, Selene allowed herself to believe it—to believe that, together, they could face whatever came next.

She didn't have to make this choice alone.

CHAPTER 13: FRACTURES

The crackling of the fire filled the silence that had settled over the Silverridge pack as they gathered around the makeshift camp. The night had fallen heavy and dark, the trees swaying gently in the cool breeze. It was a strange kind of peace after the chaos of the battle, but Selene couldn't shake the feeling of tension that still thrummed beneath the surface.

She sat on a log at the edge of the clearing, her fingers absently playing with a piece of leather, the soft glow of the fire illuminating her face. Her mind kept drifting back to the words Astrid had spoken earlier about the rogue pack's larger force. It felt like an impending storm, and no matter how much she focused on the present, she couldn't ignore the weight of it looming over them all.

And then, there was Caelan.

He had been distant since their conversation earlier. There had been no more words of comfort, no more assurances. His focus had shifted completely to the pack, to their safety, and to preparing for the inevitable war ahead. Selene couldn't help but feel a pang of hurt at the shift, though she knew it was necessary. The pack needed their Alpha to be strong, focused. But part of her—the part that had spent so much time pushing her own emotions aside—longed for that connection, that bond, that had grown between them.

"Lost in thought again?" The voice was soft, but it carried the weight of knowing.

Selene's head snapped up, and she saw Astrid standing a few feet away, her expression unreadable but her eyes sharp with concern. The Beta was always so composed, but in this moment, Selene could see the edges of tension pulling at her friend's features.

"I'm fine," Selene replied, though the words felt empty in the air. She'd said it so many times, trying to convince herself as much as anyone else.

Astrid raised an eyebrow. "You don't seem fine. I've seen that look before. It's the one you wear when you're carrying a burden you're too proud to share." She moved closer, her posture unyielding as she stood before Selene. "What's going on?"

Selene sighed and looked back at the fire. "There's too much to handle. The battle last night, the rogues closing in on us, everything..." Her voice trailed off, frustration bubbling to the surface. "And then there's Caelan."

Astrid's eyes softened, but her gaze remained fixed on Selene. "I thought you two were getting closer," she said, the words careful. "Has something changed?"

Selene hesitated, her chest tight as she wrestled with her emotions. "It feels like... he's pulling away," she admitted quietly. "He's focused on the pack, and I get it. He has to be. But it's like we're back to the way things were when we first met. He's the Alpha, and I'm just... a warrior in his pack."

Astrid's lips pressed together in a thin line. "Caelan's not like that. He never has been."

Selene frowned, looking up at her. "Then why does it feel like everything we've built between us is crumbling? It's like he's shut down again."

Astrid's gaze softened even more, her tone quiet and knowing. "You've both been through a lot. This war, the pack's survival, everything—it changes a person. It doesn't excuse pulling away, but it's not about you, Selene. Caelan's dealing with his own pressure. He's worried about losing you, about not being able to protect you, about the pack falling apart. But he won't say it. He never will."

Selene's heart sank. The words hit harder than she expected. "I just don't know if I can keep doing this," she whispered. "I don't know if I can be strong enough for him. Or for the pack."

Astrid knelt beside her, her eyes never leaving Selene's. "You don't have to be. Not alone. The strength you have comes from the people around you. From us." She paused, letting the weight of her words settle before continuing. "From him. Don't give up on him, Selene. You've both come so far. Don't let fear take that from you."

A knot tightened in Selene's throat. Astrid's words were both a balm and a challenge, and as much as Selene hated to admit it, they were true. She had spent so long alone—fighting, surviving, protecting—she didn't know how to let someone else carry the burden with her. And in this moment, she realized just how much of a fracture had formed between her and Caelan, one that she hadn't seen until now.

"Maybe I don't know how to be with him," Selene murmured. "Maybe I'm too broken."

Astrid shook her head firmly. "No. You're not broken. You're human. And so is he." She stood up, offering Selene a hand. "The only way to fix what's between you two is to face it together. Don't let fear drive you apart."

Selene looked at Astrid's hand, and after a long beat, she took it. Her fingers curled around her friend's, and as she stood, she felt a sense of clarity that had been missing. There was no magic solution, no quick fix. But the only way through this was forward. Together.

Later that night, Selene found herself at the edge of the camp, staring out into the forest. The sound of crackling flames from the fire was the only thing that broke the silence, but her mind was a whirlwind of thoughts. She knew Astrid was right. She needed to face the growing distance between herself and Caelan.

But how? How could she do that when she didn't know if they were still on the same path? How could she approach him after everything that had happened—everything they'd been through?

Her gaze drifted to where Caelan stood, speaking with some of the other pack members. He was a figure of command, his voice low but firm, his body rigid with purpose. Yet there was something else there, something Selene couldn't quite place. He looked different. More isolated. More distant.

Without thinking, she began to walk toward him, her heart pounding in her chest.

Caelan turned just as she reached him, his eyes locking with hers. For a moment, they stood there, neither speaking. The tension between them was thick enough to cut through, and Selene found it hard to breathe.

"You wanted to talk?" Caelan's voice was cautious, his eyes searching her face for something.

"I wanted to ask about the plan," she said, her voice steadier than she felt. "What's next for us?"

His gaze didn't waver, but there was something in his eyes that made her heart skip a beat. Was it relief? Regret? She couldn't tell.

Caelan ran a hand through his hair, the movement sharp and restless. "Next, we prepare for the rogue pack. We rally the allies, fortify the borders. It's a lot to handle, but we can't afford to waste time."

She nodded, trying to keep her voice steady. "And... what about us? What about what's between us?"

His eyes flickered, and for a moment, she thought he might turn away from her again, retreating into the role of the Alpha. But instead, his gaze softened, just a little.

"I don't know," he confessed quietly. "I'm trying to keep the pack together. Trying to make sure we survive this. But I—"

He stopped himself, looking away, his jaw tightening.

Selene stepped closer, her voice a whisper in the cool night air. "Caelan, I'm here. I want to be here with you. But you can't keep pushing me away. We need each other."

He exhaled a long breath, turning back to face her. "I don't know how to do this," he said, his voice rough. "I don't know how to lead the pack and keep you safe at the same time."

"You don't have to do it alone," she said, her voice firmer now. "We're in this together, remember?"

For a long moment, Caelan simply stared at her, his eyes filled with something deeper than words could convey. And then, slowly, he nodded.

"Together," he repeated softly.

The weight between them didn't lift entirely, but in that moment, something shifted. There was still uncertainty, still fear of the battles ahead, but there was also understanding. And for the first time in days, Selene felt a glimmer of hope.

They would face whatever came next—not as Alpha and warrior, not as just a pack—but as something more. Something that neither of them could define, but something they were both ready to build.
Together.

CHAPTER 14: THE GATHERING STORM

The sun had barely crested the horizon when Selene woke to the unmistakable sound of hurried footsteps. She lay still for a moment, her senses immediately alert to the sharp, predatory pulse of the forest around her. The pack was stirring—early risers already beginning their work, preparing for whatever the coming days would hold. The scent of damp earth filled the air as the remnants of morning fog clung to the trees. Selene pulled on her boots and fastened her leather armor, each movement automatic, though her thoughts were far from the task at hand. Her mind kept replaying the conversation she'd had with Caelan last night, the quiet admission that they didn't know what came next. He had admitted his fear—something Selene had never seen in him before. The weight of his role as Alpha was suffocating, and though she understood his burden, she wasn't sure how long she could stand by and watch him shoulder it alone.

But she had no choice. The pack was her family, and the rogues were still a threat they couldn't ignore. She had a duty to them, just as Caelan did. And in the midst of it all, she had to face the reality of their relationship—whatever that would become.

Stepping outside her tent, Selene was met with the cool morning breeze. The camp was bustling with activity as wolves and humans alike prepared for the day ahead. Astrid was organizing supplies nearby, her commanding presence keeping everyone on task. She shot Selene a glance and nodded, signaling her to come over.

As Selene approached, Astrid didn't waste any time.

"We need to talk about the plan," she said, her tone clipped but practical. "Caelan's been working with the scouts, and we've learned some things about the rogue pack. They're gathering strength faster than we anticipated. We need reinforcements if we're going to stand a chance."

Selene's stomach tightened at the mention of the rogues. Every time she thought they might be able to breathe, something new cropped up, a reminder that their fight wasn't over.

"What's the situation?" she asked, her voice steady.

"We've already sent word to the neighboring packs. But we can't trust that they'll come. The rogues are closing in on Silverridge faster than we thought, and if we don't act soon, they'll overrun the territory."

Selene nodded, a sense of urgency beginning to settle in her chest. They didn't have time to wait. The moment they hesitated, they risked losing everything.

"I'll talk to Caelan," she said. "We need to make sure we're ready. And if the other packs aren't coming, then we'll do this ourselves."

Astrid gave her a sharp look, clearly assessing her resolve. "You sure you want to go to him? He's already got a lot on his plate."

Selene didn't flinch. She'd been with Caelan through many battles. She knew the weight of the crown, the pressure that came with leading the pack. But she also knew that they couldn't afford to be distant from one another any longer.

"I need to talk to him. This can't be just about the pack. We need a plan, and we need to figure out how to move forward—together."

Astrid's expression softened, but her gaze held an edge of caution. "Don't wait too long to get through to him, Selene. He's drowning in this, and if you let him go down alone, you may lose him."

The warning stung more than it should have, but Selene kept her face neutral. She wasn't going to let that happen.

"I'll keep that in mind," she replied, her voice firm.

Caelan was standing at the far side of the camp when Selene found him, his back to her as he spoke with some of the scouts. His posture was tense, his shoulders squared with the weight of command. Selene paused for a moment, watching him from afar, the man she had come to know as both a leader and something more. He was the Alpha—unapproachable, untouchable. But she knew him better than anyone, and she wouldn't let him keep her at arm's length any longer.

Taking a steadying breath, she approached.

"Caelan," she called, her voice cutting through the murmurs of the camp.

He turned toward her, his face hardening when he saw her approach. He wasn't surprised to see her; if anything, there was a guarded look in his eyes as he shifted his weight, seemingly preparing for her words.

"Selene," he said, his tone neutral but with an underlying tension. "What is it?"

"I need to talk to you," she said, her voice steady. "About the rogues. About what comes next."

Caelan gave her a sharp nod and waved the scouts away, signaling them to continue their work. The moment they were alone, he crossed his arms, his gaze never leaving her. "I assume you've heard the reports. We're facing a force bigger than we anticipated."

Selene's chest tightened at the mention of the rogue pack. "Astrid filled me in. We need a strategy. We can't wait for reinforcements to arrive. If they don't come, we'll have to defend Silverridge on our own."

Caelan's jaw clenched at the thought. "We'll be outnumbered. They've been gathering for months, while we've barely had time to prepare."

"We don't have a choice," Selene said, her voice harder now, matching his intensity. "We've always fought for this land, for our pack. We won't let them take it from us."

There was a flicker in Caelan's eyes—something uncertain, something vulnerable. Selene could see it, just for a moment, before it was gone, buried beneath the mask of the Alpha. But it was enough for her to understand. He was afraid. Afraid of losing everything. Afraid of failing.

"I know you're trying to protect the pack, Caelan," she said softly, stepping closer. "But you don't have to do this alone. We'll face this together."

His eyes softened, but there was still a distance between them. "I can't risk your safety," he muttered. "Not now. Not when the rogues are this close."

Selene took another step forward, until there was nothing but a hair's breadth between them. She could feel the heat of his body, the tension in the air between them. She could feel how he pulled back, how he kept his walls up. But she wasn't going to back down.

"You don't have to protect me, Caelan. We protect each other. That's what this is about. That's what it's always been about."

He exhaled sharply, his gaze faltering for just a fraction of a second before he regained control. "I don't know how to do that, Selene," he admitted quietly. "I don't know how to balance being your Alpha and being… with you."

Selene felt her heart skip a beat. "I know it's hard. But we don't have to have it all figured out. We just need to be in this together."

For a long moment, Caelan didn't speak. He stood there, as if weighing her words against the storm of responsibility that raged inside him. Selene waited, her heart pounding, the weight of the situation pressing in on her.

Finally, he stepped forward, his hands reaching for her. His touch was hesitant at first, as though afraid she might pull away, but when she didn't, he pulled her into his arms. The feeling of his strength enveloping her, the steady rhythm of his heartbeat against hers, grounded her in a way nothing else could.

"I don't want to lose you, Selene," he murmured against her hair. "I don't know what's coming next. But I know I don't want to face it without you."

Her breath caught in her throat as she tilted her head back to meet his gaze. "You won't lose me," she said, her voice steady. "Not now, not ever."

For the first time in what felt like forever, Caelan's walls cracked. His gaze softened, the tension in his posture slowly unwinding.

"We'll face it together," he agreed, his voice thick with emotion.

Selene nodded, her chest swelling with a quiet sense of relief. The battle ahead would be brutal, and the rogue threat was still very real. But in that moment, they had each other. And that was more than enough to face whatever came next.

As the day wore on, the Silverridge pack gathered for the final briefing. The air was thick with determination and resolve. They had no time to waste. The rogue force was coming, and they had to be ready.

But as Selene looked around at the faces of the wolves she had sworn to protect, she realized one thing: they weren't alone. They were a family. And together, they would fight until the end.

The storm was coming. But they would stand against it— unbroken, united.

CHAPTER 15: THE CALM BEFORE THE STORM

The evening air was thick with the scent of pine and earth, the last traces of sunlight filtering through the dense trees, casting long shadows over the camp. The Silverridge pack had spent the day reinforcing their defenses, making final preparations for the inevitable clash with the rogue pack. Selene stood at the edge of the clearing, watching the sunset with a heavy heart. There was something in the air tonight—a strange stillness. It was as if the forest itself held its breath, waiting for the storm to come. The weight of the situation pressed down on her chest, and for the first time in days, she felt the cold sting of fear. Not for herself, but for the pack, for Caelan. She had seen the stress in his eyes, the burden of leadership bearing down on him. He was the Alpha, but even he couldn't carry the weight alone.

The thought of the rogue pack, their numbers growing stronger each day, made her stomach turn. She knew they would fight with everything they had, but even that might not be enough. The unknown loomed in front of them, and as much as they had prepared, there were too many variables they couldn't control.

"Selene," a soft voice broke through her thoughts.

She turned to see Caelan walking toward her, his expression unreadable but his presence undeniable. The way he moved through the camp—calm, deliberate, with that air of authority that came naturally to him—was a reminder of the man he had become. The Alpha.

"I was looking for you," he said, his voice low but steady. "We need to discuss the final plans."

Selene nodded, her heart tightening as she met his gaze. There was something about him tonight—a quiet intensity that made her chest ache. She knew what was coming. She knew that, regardless of how prepared they were, this battle would change everything.

"Let's go over the details then," she said, trying to keep her voice steady.

Caelan led her to a small gathering near the center of the camp, where Astrid and several other trusted pack members were waiting. Maps were spread out on a wooden table, the crude lines marking the borders, the known locations of rogue activity, and key strategic points. The pack had spent hours strategizing, but now the time had come to put it all into motion.

Astrid looked up as they approached, her sharp eyes immediately assessing Selene's mood. Without a word, she handed her a piece of parchment with the latest reports.

"Caelan's been running point on this, but we need to finalize everything," Astrid said, her tone clipped but efficient. "The rogues are moving fast, but we still have a small window to prepare."

Selene took the parchment, scanning the figures and locations. She could feel Caelan's presence beside her, his silent support like a weight against her side. He didn't speak at first, his eyes focused on the map, but she could feel the tension rolling off him in waves. The Alpha. Always holding it together, always carrying the pack's burdens.

She felt a pang of empathy. She wanted to help him, wanted to share that burden, but she knew this was something only he could carry.

"I'll take the northern front with the scouts," Selene said, breaking the silence. "We can delay them if we set up early warning systems and fall back to the second line of defense if necessary."

Astrid nodded approvingly, her sharp gaze flicking between them. "That's the plan. We'll hold the eastern border with the main force, and if they push through, we'll have reserves to flank them."

Caelan remained quiet for a moment before speaking, his voice measured but heavy. "The rogues are more organized than we expected. They know our terrain, they know our weaknesses. We can't afford to underestimate them."

Selene's gaze met his, the unspoken understanding between them clear. He wasn't just talking about the battle. He was talking about everything—the pressure of leading, the weight of keeping the pack safe. She could see it in the tightness of his jaw, the subtle strain in his posture.

"We won't let them break us," Selene said, her voice strong. "We'll fight together. We'll hold them off."

Caelan's eyes softened for a moment, the flicker of something vulnerable passing through them. But just as quickly, it was gone, buried beneath the mask of the Alpha. He nodded sharply.

"You're right. We stand together. And we win this together."

Later that evening, after the final strategy had been set, Selene found herself standing at the edge of the camp again, this time alone. The firelight flickered in the distance, casting long, wavering shadows over the clearing. The sound of voices was distant, the pack members preparing for the battle to come. But here, in this moment, it felt as though the world had quieted down.

The weight of what was about to happen pressed heavily on her chest. She had faced many battles before, but none like this. The rogue pack wasn't just a group of mindless enemies—they were coordinated, ruthless, and they wanted the Silverridge pack's territory. They wanted everything Caelan had built.

And she couldn't help but feel a chill of uncertainty. Would they be enough to stop them? Would they be able to protect the pack? Caelan was counting on her, and she couldn't let him down. She couldn't let the pack down.

"Selene," came a familiar voice, pulling her from her thoughts. She turned to see Caelan approaching, his face softer than it had been earlier, though the tension still lingered in his posture.

"You shouldn't be out here alone," he said, his tone gentle but concerned.

She met his gaze, feeling the warmth of his presence grounding her. She smiled faintly, though it didn't reach her eyes. "Just needed a moment to clear my head."

Caelan stepped closer, his hand brushing hers for a brief moment before he wrapped it around her wrist, pulling her gently to face him. "I know. We've all needed that. But we have to be ready for what's coming."

"I'm ready," she said quietly, though the uncertainty still lingered in her chest. "We all are."

He didn't respond right away, his eyes searching hers. There was something in his gaze, something that made her heart race, something almost... desperate. But before she could voice the question that hovered on the tip of her tongue, he spoke again.

"Selene, I—" He broke off, clearly struggling with something. "I need you to know something."

She frowned, instinctively stepping closer. "What is it?"

Caelan exhaled slowly, his grip tightening around her wrist as he pulled her a little closer, his forehead resting against hers for a brief moment. "I need you to know that no matter what happens tomorrow... I couldn't do this without you. I couldn't lead this pack without you by my side."

Her breath caught in her throat. She had always known that Caelan cared for her, but hearing it—hearing him say it—hit her harder than she had expected. The vulnerability in his voice, the unspoken truth in his words, made her heart swell.

"You won't lose me," she whispered, her voice thick with emotion. "Not now. Not ever."

Caelan's gaze softened, his eyes locking onto hers with an intensity that made her pulse quicken. He leaned down slightly, as if tempted to kiss her, but he stopped just short, his lips brushing against her forehead in a gentle, lingering touch.

"I can't afford to lose you," he murmured. "I'm not sure what I'd do if I did."

Selene's heart hammered in her chest as she reached up to touch his face. The moment felt suspended in time, fragile and full of promise. She didn't know what the next day would bring, what the battle would cost them, but in that moment, she knew they would face it together. No matter what happened, they were a team.

The calm before the storm felt like a lifetime, but as the last light of day faded into the deep blues of night, Selene finally allowed herself to believe in the one thing she had never let herself fully embrace: hope.

Together, they would face the storm. Together, they would fight for their pack, for each other.

And no matter what the future held, they would not break.

The night passed in a blur of preparation, quiet conversations, and final goodbyes. But beneath it all, a sense of resolve hung in the air. The Silverridge pack would stand strong, and they would fight until the very end.

As Selene lay in her tent later that night, the weight of the battle ahead pressing heavily on her, she finally allowed herself to close her eyes and rest. Tomorrow, the fight would begin. But for now, she allowed herself a moment of peace. For tomorrow, the storm would come.

CHAPTER 16: THE BATTLE BEGINS

The air was cold and thick with the scent of rain as Selene stood at the edge of the camp, her eyes scanning the horizon. The sounds of the pack preparing for battle filled the air—voices low, hurried, and filled with a sense of purpose. This was it. The moment they had been preparing for, the storm they had all known was coming.

Her heart beat heavily in her chest as she tightened the straps on her armor. The night had been restless, and despite her best efforts to sleep, her mind had raced with thoughts of the battle, the pack, and Caelan. She couldn't shake the weight of the responsibility that was now resting on all their shoulders.

Beside her, Astrid was organizing the final details with a sharp efficiency that was both reassuring and terrifying. The older woman had always been the rock of the Silverridge pack—calm, collected, and always ready with a plan. But even Astrid's cool demeanor couldn't hide the tension in her movements today.

"We're ready," Astrid said, glancing at Selene. "It's time."

Selene nodded, but her mind kept drifting back to Caelan. She hadn't seen him since their conversation last night, and a part of her wondered if he was holding up as well as he seemed. The weight of leadership wasn't just on his shoulders—it was on his heart as well. She knew that better than anyone. And she couldn't help but feel that this battle wasn't just about the survival of the pack. It was about something deeper—a test of trust, of sacrifice, and of their bond.

"I'll meet you at the eastern border," Selene said, giving Astrid a final nod before heading toward the clearing where the wolves were gathering.

The camp had transformed from a haven into a battlefield overnight. Every wolf was in formation, ready for the oncoming attack. The air was thick with anticipation, and

despite their preparation, there was an undeniable tension that hung over them like a cloud, a sense of foreboding that couldn't be shaken off.
As Selene made her way through the camp, she caught sight of Caelan. He was standing near the center, surrounded by the rest of the pack's leaders. His face was hard and unreadable, his jaw clenched in determination. But when his eyes met hers, something softened in them—a flicker of something deep, something unspoken.
"Selene," he said, his voice low but steady, as she approached. "You're ready?"
She nodded, her heart fluttering nervously in her chest. "We're ready. Are you?"
Caelan gave a tight, almost imperceptible nod. "I have to be." There was an edge to his words, a sharpness that came from carrying the burden of command. But beneath that, there was something else—a vulnerability she had seen in him only a few times before, and it only made her more determined to fight by his side.
"I'll be right there with you," Selene said, her voice firm, reaching out to briefly touch his arm. "We'll get through this together."
Caelan's gaze softened for a moment, and his hand reached up to squeeze hers, a silent promise that they were not alone in this.
"Together," he agreed.

The first signs of the rogue pack came in the early morning light. By the time the sun had fully risen, the Silverridge pack had already taken their positions along the borders of the territory. The scouts had spotted the rogue forces advancing through the trees, their numbers greater than they had feared.
"They're moving faster than we expected," Astrid reported, her eyes scanning the tree line. "It's going to be a full-on assault."
Selene nodded, her hand resting on the hilt of her sword. "We won't let them through. We hold the line."

Caelan's voice came from behind her, calm but edged with authority. "You're with the northern group. We'll need to push them back, slow them down. If we can break their formation, we'll have a chance."

Selene turned to face him, meeting his gaze. "What about you?"

Caelan's jaw clenched, but he didn't hesitate. "I'll be in the thick of it. I need to lead the charge. But I'll watch your back."

Her heart skipped a beat. He was always so determined, always so focused on the pack's survival. But there was something more in his words, something that made her heart ache. He needed her by his side—not just as his packmate, but as his partner.

"Be safe," she said quietly, and though it was a simple request, it carried the weight of everything they had been through together.

Caelan smiled, but it didn't quite reach his eyes. "You too."

The battle began with a sudden roar of chaos. The first wave of the rogue pack slammed into the defensive line with terrifying force. Selene's instincts kicked in immediately, her body moving with fluid precision as she fought alongside the rest of the pack. She could feel the energy of the pack around her, the shared determination that bound them all together. Every strike, every movement, was coordinated, like an extension of herself.

But it wasn't enough. The rogues were relentless, their numbers overwhelming. For every rogue that fell, another seemed to take their place. Selene's breath came in sharp gasps as she sliced through an attacker, her sword cutting through the air with a deadly grace. She barely registered the pain in her side as she fought on, adrenaline pushing her forward.

She caught a glimpse of Caelan in the thick of the battle—his form unmistakable as he fought fiercely, taking down rogue after rogue with brutal precision. His wolf was out, a massive force of power and rage, as he tore through the enemy lines.

But the rogues weren't just fighting for territory—they were fighting to break the pack, to tear apart everything Silverridge stood for. And it was clear that they were willing to sacrifice everything to do it.

"Push them back!" Selene shouted, her voice cutting through the chaos as she and the other wolves pressed forward, forcing the rogues to retreat.

The battle raged on, each moment feeling like an eternity. The sounds of snarling wolves, clashing weapons, and shouts filled the air, but beneath it all, there was something primal, something raw. This wasn't just a fight for survival—it was a fight for everything they had built.

Selene's arms were heavy with exhaustion, and her energy was beginning to wane. But she couldn't stop. She wouldn't. Not when so much was at stake.

Then, as if the universe had decided they had fought enough, a new force appeared on the horizon.

"A second wave," Astrid yelled, her voice full of dread.

Selene's heart sank. They had anticipated the rogues would send reinforcements, but not this quickly. The battle was shifting, and they were starting to lose ground.

"Fall back to the secondary line!" Caelan's commanding voice rang out over the battlefield, cutting through the noise.

The pack responded immediately, retreating in an organized, disciplined fashion, but even as they fell back, the pressure of the rogue pack's advance was suffocating.

Selene kept moving, her sword held tightly in her hand as she watched Caelan lead the retreat, his presence as commanding as ever. But the worry in his eyes couldn't be hidden. The battle was turning against them, and they didn't have the numbers to sustain it.

"Get to the rear!" Selene shouted at the others, ushering them toward safety as she worked her way through the fray. She had to get to Caelan.

But before she could make her way to the front, something caught her eye. A rogue, larger and more vicious than the rest, was advancing on Caelan. His eyes locked onto her, and she could see the hunger in his gaze, the intent to take down the Alpha.

"Caelan!" Selene shouted, her heart racing.

He turned, just in time to meet the rogue's challenge, but the brute's strength was overwhelming. Caelan was pushed back, and for a moment, Selene's blood ran cold. She couldn't let this happen. Not now. Not when everything depended on them.

With a snarl, she lunged forward, her sword aimed directly for the rogue's back. But before she could reach him, a blur of movement—an immense force—tore the rogue off Caelan, sending him crashing to the ground.

It was Caelan. His wolf had taken over completely, his massive form a blur of muscle and fury as he tore into the rogue with savage speed.

Selene stopped, her breath catching in her throat as she watched the Alpha fight for his life, for their future. She didn't need words. She knew the battle was far from over. But together, they would fight until the very end.

And they would win.

No matter what.

CHAPTER 17: THE TIDE TURNS

The battle had become a blur. The clash of steel against fur, the roar of wolves, the grunts of exertion and pain, all blending together in a cacophony of chaos. For Selene, time had stopped. She was lost in the fight, every instinct focused on survival, on the safety of the pack, and on keeping her promise to Caelan. They had fought for this land, for this pack, and they would not let it slip away.

She could feel the burn of exhaustion in her muscles, the sting of her wounds as they began to bleed through her armor. The rogues were relentless, pushing forward with a fury that threatened to overwhelm them. Despite their best efforts, the Silverridge pack was being pushed back further, the ground gained by the rogues impossible to reclaim. Selene's breath came in harsh gasps, but her focus never wavered. She was part of something greater now, bound to the pack, to Caelan, and to the land they swore to protect. She couldn't afford to falter. Not when so much was on the line.

"Selene!" Astrid's voice broke through the madness.

Selene turned to find the older woman fighting her way toward her, her face smeared with blood but her eyes sharp and calculating.

"We need to fall back," Astrid said, urgency in her voice. "They're too strong. We can't keep this up much longer."

Selene's heart sank. She had known the battle was turning, but hearing it from Astrid—the one person who never flinched under pressure—made it real. They were losing. And they needed to regroup, or they would be wiped out entirely.

But Selene wasn't ready to give up. Not yet. She glanced toward the center of the battle, where Caelan's massive wolf form was still tearing through the enemy. He was a force of nature, unstoppable, but even he couldn't hold back the tide alone.

"I won't leave him," Selene said, her voice hard. "We need to turn the tide. If we push back the eastern flank, we can buy time."

Astrid frowned, clearly torn between strategy and loyalty. "You're risking too much. You're already exhausted."

"I won't let them fall," Selene replied, her voice low but resolute. "Not now. Not when it's this close."

Astrid's eyes studied her for a long moment before she gave a sharp nod. "Then we'll do it together. We don't have time to waste."

Without another word, Selene and Astrid turned toward the front lines, their blades flashing in the dim light as they fought their way through the chaos. The eastern flank was where the rogue's main force had focused their assault, and it was now the pack's weak point. If they couldn't break through, they would be surrounded, and the pack would have no way to escape.

They fought side by side, cutting through the rogue ranks with precision, their movements a deadly dance. Selene's muscles screamed with fatigue, but she pushed past it, blocking a rogue's strike before stabbing her sword through his chest. She didn't pause to see him fall—she couldn't afford to. There was no time for hesitation.

The more they fought, the more she realized how dire the situation truly was. The rogues weren't just organized; they were relentless, and they seemed to be everywhere. And with every passing minute, the line between victory and defeat blurred more and more.

"Hold the line!" Caelan's voice rang out over the battlefield, his commanding tone cutting through the noise like a whip. He was still fighting in his wolf form, his massive body a blur of fur and muscle as he tore through rogue after rogue. But even his strength had its limits.

Selene's eyes locked onto him. He was the heart of the pack, and they needed him alive. He couldn't fall, not when they were so close to the end.

Her breath hitched in her throat as she watched him take down another rogue. But as his wolf form turned to strike again, he was met by a massive opponent—a rogue Alpha, larger and more powerful than the others. The rogue Alpha's clawed hand swiped through the air, hitting Caelan hard across the side, sending him crashing to the ground with a bone-rattling thud.

"Caelan!" Selene screamed, her voice filled with a sharp, raw panic that cut through her fear. Her heart skipped a beat as she rushed forward, cutting through the remaining rogues that stood between her and him.

Caelan's wolf was struggling to rise, his massive form battered and bruised. He shook his head violently, trying to clear the disorientation caused by the hit, but the rogue Alpha was already on top of him, slashing down with claws that could rend flesh and bone.

No. Not now. Not when they had come so far.

With a snarl, Selene pushed herself forward, her sword raised high. She had no choice. She couldn't allow Caelan to fall. Not like this.

The rogue Alpha turned just in time to see her coming. His eyes flicked to her, and in that moment, Selene saw something more than the fury of battle in his gaze—there was a cold calculation, a challenge. This rogue Alpha wanted Caelan's position. He wanted his power.

But Selene would not let him take it. Not without a fight.

She dove into the fray, her sword slashing toward the rogue Alpha's throat. The rogue twisted, raising his arm to block, but Selene was faster, her strike landing deep into the muscle of his arm. The rogue Alpha howled in pain, staggering back, but it wasn't enough to deter him.

He turned on her with a vicious growl, his claws swiping down at her. Selene leapt to the side, narrowly avoiding the strike, but she could feel the rush of air as the rogue's claws tore past her. She gritted her teeth, ignoring the panic rising in her chest.

Before the rogue Alpha could recover, Caelan lunged. His wolf form exploded forward with all the fury of an Alpha, his massive jaws clamping around the rogue's throat. There was

a sickening crack, followed by a strangled howl, and then the rogue fell silent, his body limp in Caelan's powerful grip.
Caelan stood over him, breathing heavily, his fur matted with blood. His eyes met Selene's, his gaze intense and filled with gratitude and something more—something raw and vulnerable.
"Thank you," he whispered, his voice breaking through the madness around them.
Selene didn't respond with words. Instead, she stepped toward him, her hand reaching for his. She knew what he was trying to say—she had seen it in his eyes before. The bond between them was more than just a shared love for the pack. It was something deeper, something unspoken, that had been building for weeks.
She squeezed his hand tightly, her heart soaring with relief that he was still standing, still fighting. Together, they could win this. Together, they could do anything.
"We're not done yet," Selene said, her voice steady despite the turmoil raging inside her.
Caelan nodded, a determined gleam in his eyes. "Let's finish this."

The tides had turned. The Silverridge pack had begun to regain ground, pushing back against the rogue forces. With their Alpha and his mate leading the charge, they rallied, and one by one, the rogues began to fall. Their resolve shattered as the strength of the pack came back with renewed fury.
Selene fought with everything she had, her energy returning with the knowledge that victory was within their grasp. The rogue Alpha's death had struck a blow to their morale, and now, it was only a matter of time before the last of the rogues were driven out.
As the final waves of battle drew to a close, Selene stood beside Caelan, their hands entwined, their bodies bruised and bloodied but unbroken.
"We did it," Selene whispered, her voice filled with awe.
Caelan's gaze softened, and he nodded. "Together."
And with that, the storm passed. The battle was over.

But the war was far from finished.

CHAPTER 18: SHATTERED ILLUSIONS

The battle was over, but the cost of victory had left a bitter taste in Selene's mouth. The bodies of the fallen—rogues and packmates alike—littered the ground, a grim reminder of what they had endured. The Silverridge pack had survived, but the landscape had been irreversibly changed. It wasn't just the land that had been scarred, but the hearts of those who had fought to protect it.

Selene sat on a large rock, her back stiff from the fight, staring into the distance. The scent of blood still hung in the air, the aftershocks of the battle vibrating through her body like an endless pulse. She tried to focus on the small victories—on the fact that they had defended their territory, that the rogues had been driven out—but her mind kept drifting back to the faces of the fallen, to the ones they hadn't been able to save.

"Selene."

Caelan's voice was a deep, comforting presence in the aftermath, but there was something in it that made her look up sharply. When she turned to face him, she saw the tightness around his eyes—the weight of the battle had settled on him, too. His hair was matted with blood, and there was a faint limp in his step as he approached.

She stood up, brushing the dirt from her pants, though the movement was automatic. Her body was still buzzing with adrenaline, but she knew it wouldn't last much longer. The exhaustion would hit her soon enough, like a wave crashing into the shore.

He looked at her with something close to frustration in his gaze, though it was tempered with concern. "We need to talk."

Her heart sank. She had felt the distance between them growing ever since the battle began, but she wasn't sure how to bridge it. There was something different in his eyes now, something that had been absent before. She opened her mouth to respond, but he cut her off.

"Not here," he said, glancing around them, where their pack members were beginning to tend to the wounded and clean up the mess left in the wake of the battle. "Come with me."

They walked in silence through the woods, the only sound between them the crunch of leaves beneath their feet and the distant cries of wolves as they mourned the loss of their fallen comrades. Selene's mind raced with a thousand questions, but none of them seemed to matter as much as the tension that hung thick in the air. Caelan had always been open with her—at least, that's how it had felt before. But now, as they walked deeper into the forest, it felt like a rift was forming between them.

When they reached a small clearing, Caelan turned to face her. The dim light of the setting sun cast long shadows, and Selene could see the strain in his posture, the way he clenched his fists at his sides as if trying to hold himself together. She took a deep breath, waiting for him to speak, knowing that the next few moments would change everything.

"I—" Caelan began, his voice rough, almost apologetic, but he stopped himself, his jaw tightening. He ran a hand through his hair, then looked at her with a kind of determination. "You've seen it, haven't you?"

Selene tilted her head, confusion furrowing her brow. "Seen what?"

"The way I've been acting," he said, the words coming out in a rush, as if he couldn't contain them any longer. "Ever since the rogues first appeared, I've been... distant. And now, after all of this, I can't ignore it anymore."

She swallowed, her throat tightening. "Caelan, what are you saying?"

He let out a breath, his gaze flickering away for a moment before meeting hers with intensity. "I haven't been fair to you. Not in the way I should have been. I've kept pushing you away, and I know that. But it's more than just that."

Selene's heart began to pound in her chest, the weight of his words sinking in slowly, painfully. "Caelan…" she whispered, feeling the ache in her chest deepen.

"I—I can't stop thinking about her," he said, the words tumbling out like a confession. "My destined mate. I've tried to ignore it, but it's always there. Every time I look at you, I feel like I'm betraying her."

The world seemed to tilt on its axis, and for a long moment, Selene couldn't find her voice. She had known this was coming—had felt it like a shadow hanging over them. The bond he shared with his destined mate had been the one thing that had always stood between them, and now, it seemed, it was finally breaking them apart.

"Caelan," Selene said softly, taking a step back, her heart constricting as the reality of the situation crashed down on her. "I—I don't understand. What are you saying? That you're going to choose her over me?"

He flinched at her words, his eyes darkening with guilt. "I don't want to," he admitted, his voice rough. "But I don't know how to ignore it anymore. I can't. It's like a pull, something I can't break, no matter how hard I try."

Selene's chest ached as if a part of her were being ripped away. She knew this was always the danger of their relationship—she had always known that his destined mate would come into the picture one day, that she would have to share him with someone else. But to hear him admit it, to see the conflict in his eyes, made it all too real.

"You've made your choice, then," she said, her voice barely a whisper, but the hurt in it was undeniable. "You're choosing her."

Caelan reached out, his expression pained, but she stepped back, shaking her head. "You don't get it, Caelan. You can't just expect me to stand by while you go off to be with someone else. I love you. I've always loved you. But this… this is too much."

"I never meant to hurt you," he said, his voice breaking slightly. "I care about you, Selene. I don't want to lose you, but I don't know what else to do. The bond with her is too strong, and it's tearing me apart."

Selene felt the tears welling in her eyes, but she blinked them away angrily. She wasn't going to cry over this. She wasn't going to let him see how much his words had shattered her.

"You should have thought of that before," she said, her voice trembling despite her best efforts to remain strong. "Before you dragged me into this. Before you made me believe that we could have something real."

She turned away from him, her heart pounding in her chest. "I need space, Caelan. I need time to think."

He reached out again, but this time, she didn't stop. She couldn't stop. Not when everything she had believed in was falling apart around her.

"Selene, please don't—" he began, but she was already walking away, her feet carrying her through the woods, away from the man she loved, away from the pack, away from everything that had once felt like home.

And with every step she took, a part of her felt like she was leaving him behind for good.

CHAPTER 19: THE BREAKING POINT

Selene didn't stop walking. She didn't look back, even when the crunch of Caelan's footsteps behind her faded into the distance. Her breath came in shallow, uneven gasps, her heart thudding in her chest as she pushed herself further into the woods. The world felt muffled now, distant, as if everything around her had slowed to a crawl.

Her mind was a whirlpool of emotion, each thought tumbling over the other, drowning her in a tide of confusion and pain. How had it come to this? She had fought for him, bled for him, and yet, here she was—abandoned in every sense of the word.

The pain in her chest, raw and suffocating, was so overwhelming that it was almost a physical ache. She had known about his destined mate, knew the pull that existed between them, but she had always believed in their bond—believed that it was strong enough to hold them together. She had trusted Caelan, trusted that his feelings for her weren't fleeting. But now, standing in the cold quiet of the forest, she realized that she had been fooling herself all along.

Her feet faltered, her body trembling as she leaned against a tree, trying to steady herself. Her fingers dug into the rough bark as she took deep breaths, forcing herself to regain control, but it was impossible. The tears she had refused to shed in front of Caelan fell freely now, streaking down her face like tiny rivers of hurt.

"You can't do this, Selene," she whispered to herself. "You can't keep running."

But the reality of it was, she didn't know how to stay.

She didn't know how to stay with someone who had already made his choice.

The hours stretched on, the sun sinking lower into the sky, casting the world in shades of orange and pink. Selene was aware of time passing, but it didn't matter. Every minute felt like an eternity, a reminder of everything she had lost. She hadn't eaten. She hadn't drunk anything. All she could think about was the last conversation with Caelan—the words that had shattered everything.

The pull of her emotions was so strong that it felt like the weight of the world was pressing down on her shoulders. She couldn't breathe. She couldn't think straight. Every thought of Caelan made her chest tighten with the strangest mixture of longing and anger. *How could he choose her over me? How could he choose anyone over me?*

Eventually, she found herself at the edge of the forest, where the trees began to thin out. Her vision blurred, the weight of her exhaustion catching up to her, and her body trembled with the strain of everything she had endured since the battle. She needed to sit, to rest, to escape the hurt that was threatening to consume her. But just as she turned to find a place to collapse, she heard something—someone—behind her.

"Selene?"

She stiffened, her heart stuttering in her chest as her eyes flew to the voice. And there, standing at the edge of the clearing, was Kael.

The sight of him—a rogue who had once been part of the Silverridge pack, but who had broken away after the previous Alpha's fall—made her heart throb painfully in her chest. Kael had been a part of her past. He had always been there, on the fringes, watching. But there was no denying the undeniable chemistry between them.

"Kael?" she asked, her voice hoarse. "What are you doing here?"

He took a cautious step forward, his eyes scanning her face with concern. "I heard the battle was over, and... well, I knew I'd find you out here."

Selene felt her brows furrow in confusion. "What are you talking about?"

Kael's face softened, his gaze sincere. "I know you're hurting," he said, his voice steady but laced with an unmistakable undercurrent of care. "And I know you're confused. But you don't have to do this alone, Selene."

She clenched her jaw, fighting the urge to turn away, to push him out of her life completely. She didn't want anyone near her right now—not Kael, not Caelan, not anyone. Her heart was too broken to let anyone else in.

"I'm not confused," she said bitterly. "I'm just... done. I'm done with all of it. The lies, the betrayal. I thought... I thought I was enough, Kael. But I wasn't. And that's something I need to come to terms with."

Kael's expression softened further, his eyes flashing with empathy. "I know how it feels to be discarded," he said quietly, "To be left behind by the ones you love. I've been there. But you don't have to carry this burden by yourself."

"Why should I trust you?" Selene's voice broke with the weight of her own disillusionment. "You left too. You chose to leave, to walk away."

Kael stepped closer, his eyes intense but calm. "Because, unlike Caelan, I never left you, Selene. I never stopped thinking about you. I—"

Before he could continue, Selene shook her head, her hand rising to stop him. "Kael, please. I don't want to hear it."

But Kael didn't back away. Instead, he reached out, his hand brushing her cheek in a gesture that was both gentle and familiar, a silent promise of comfort.

"I never wanted to hurt you, Selene. I know what you've been through. I know you're in pain right now, but you don't have to do this alone. I'm still here. I've always been here."

Selene's breath caught in her throat. The warmth of his touch was comforting, but it also felt like another layer of betrayal. She didn't want him here. Not now, not when her heart was already shredded. But as she looked into his eyes, the weight of her isolation and grief hit her like a tidal wave.

For a long moment, there was nothing but the silent understanding between them, and for the first time since Caelan's words had broken her, Selene felt a small, fleeting comfort. Maybe Kael wasn't the answer, but for now, he was the only one who understood what it felt like to be left behind.

"Why do you keep trying to save me?" she whispered, her voice barely audible as she leaned into his touch. "After everything?"

Kael's eyes were soft, filled with something like sorrow. "Because I care about you, Selene. I always have."

Her heart thudded in her chest, conflicted. She wasn't ready to forgive, wasn't ready to move on—but as she stood there with Kael, something inside her whispered that maybe she didn't have to make a decision just yet. Maybe she could find solace here, for a little while, until she had the strength to figure out what her heart truly wanted.

And with that thought, Selene allowed herself to close her eyes, to rest, to let Kael's presence offer the briefest sense of peace. But deep down, she knew this wasn't the end. This was just another chapter in the broken story of her heart.

The evening was quiet, the stars above hidden behind thick clouds, but Selene's heart beat loudly in the stillness of the night.

CHAPTER 20: A NEW BEGINNING

The days after that moment with Kael had blurred together in a haze. Time moved forward, but for Selene, it felt like she was stuck in limbo. She had allowed herself to rest, to lean on Kael's comforting presence, but the pain in her chest never truly went away. It lingered, gnawing at her, reminding her of everything she had lost. Of everything Caelan had taken from her.
The Silverridge pack had slowly started to heal from the aftermath of the rogue battle. The injured were recovering, the fallen mourned, and the wounds of the fight were slowly beginning to fade into the background, overshadowed by the tension within the pack, and with her.
Caelan had made no attempt to find her after that night. His silence was its own kind of betrayal, a reminder of his choice—of his departure from her. Every day that passed without him seeking her out only solidified the truth that she was no longer a part of his future. She had expected as much, but the realization still cut like a knife.
But it was time to move on.
The forest behind her had become a sanctuary, but the longer she stayed in isolation, the more the weight of her grief pressed down on her. She could feel the eyes of the pack upon her—sympathy, curiosity, and quiet judgment in their gaze. The whispers had died down, but they hadn't disappeared. Some of the pack were still divided. There were those who supported Caelan, who understood his need to honor the bond with his destined mate, and then there were those who looked at Selene with pity, as if she had been nothing more than a fleeting distraction in his life.
She wasn't going to let them define her. She wasn't going to let her pain dictate who she was.
It was time to step forward.

The clearing in front of her, where the pack had often gathered for meetings and celebrations, was quiet. The tension between the remaining Alpha and his intended mate had left a heavy air behind, but the space had become a symbol of the pack's resilience. It was where they came together to heal, to make decisions, and to face the future as a unit.

Today, Selene stood in the center of the clearing, alone. She had chosen this moment, this space, to make a declaration—not just for herself, but for the entire pack. She had been their Beta once, and she was still a part of them, in a way. The love she'd felt for them, for her pack, hadn't disappeared simply because her bond with Caelan had been shattered.

Her back straightened, her gaze sweeping over the trees, the horizon, as the first rays of the sun broke through the canopy. The world felt full of potential, full of quiet promise.

There was a stirring behind her, the low rumble of footsteps, and she didn't need to turn around to know who it was. She'd felt his presence before he spoke, before he stepped into her line of sight.

"Selene," Kael's voice called, steady, warm. She glanced over her shoulder, and his eyes softened when he met her gaze. "I didn't know if you were coming."

"I'm here," she said, her voice clear. She turned to face him fully, her body steadying as she took a deep breath. "And I'm not going anywhere."

Kael nodded, his lips curling into a small, understanding smile. He stepped forward, stopping just in front of her, but giving her space. He knew—just as she did—that this was her moment to take back control. To decide what came next, both for herself and for the pack.

"This isn't over yet, is it?" Kael said softly, his gaze flickering to the distance where the pack members were slowly gathering.

"No," she replied, shaking her head. "It's just beginning."

She could feel it now—the change in the air, in herself. The grief had its place, but it no longer defined her. She had the strength to move on. She wasn't Caelan's second choice. She wasn't anyone's consolation prize. She was Selene, Beta of the Silverridge pack, and she had a future to fight for. Her future. Her own path.

Kael gave her a small nod, as though understanding the silent vow she had made. He stepped back, allowing her to lead the next part of this journey. His presence, though comforting, was no longer something she needed to lean on. She had found the strength within herself, and that was what mattered.

One by one, the pack began to gather in the clearing, their expressions a mix of curiosity and cautious hope. She could feel their eyes on her—expectation, but no judgment. The pack needed her now, and she would not fail them.

She raised her voice, steady and sure. "Silverridge pack," she began, the words coming easily, the weight of them filling the space. "You have all fought for this pack. You have bled for it. You have lost, and you have triumphed. And now it's time for us to move forward. We will not be defined by our losses. We will not be broken by the past."

Her eyes swept over them all, making sure they saw the fire in her gaze, the unwavering strength that burned there.

"We have a future to build. Together. We don't need to rely on a single Alpha. We don't need to live in the shadows of past mistakes. I am here. I am still your Beta, and I will help lead this pack into the future we deserve."

The murmurs of the pack began, low at first, before it built into something louder, stronger. They were listening. They were understanding. And in that moment, she knew that they were with her.

Behind her, she heard the sound of footsteps. Caelan's footsteps.

The Alpha of the Silverridge pack had arrived.

But Selene didn't look back. She didn't need to. She knew he was there, but the focus had shifted. She had shifted. The pack had shifted.

Caelan's voice was quiet, almost apologetic, but she didn't need to hear it. "Selene, I…"

"I'm not the woman you left behind," she said, her words cutting through the air, strong and final. "I'm not the woman who needs you anymore."

The silence that followed wasn't uncomfortable—it was a weight being lifted. Caelan didn't speak again. There was nothing else to say. He had made his choice, and she had made hers.

The pack began to stir, whispering, exchanging glances. The future of Silverridge wasn't dependent on Caelan or his bond with his destined mate. It was theirs to shape, theirs to fight for.

And as Selene stood there, a quiet strength growing within her, she realized that for the first time in a long time, she wasn't alone. She had her pack. She had herself. And that was more than enough.

With a final glance at Caelan, she turned away. The clearing was filled with voices, filled with hope.

And it was enough.

As Selene walked forward, her steps were sure, her path clear. The future of the Silverridge pack was uncertain, but for the first time, she was ready to face it.

Alone, but not really alone.

She had everything she needed within herself.

CHAPTER 21: THE PATH AHEAD

The first few weeks after that moment in the clearing felt like a slow unraveling of everything Selene had once thought she knew about herself, about the pack, and about the future she had envisioned with Caelan. She had spent years as a part of Silverridge, standing by his side, helping him lead, giving everything she had to the pack. The weight of their bond had once felt like a solid foundation, something she could rely on, something that defined her purpose.

Now, she was learning to redefine herself.

As Beta, Selene had never been one to shy away from responsibility, and now, more than ever, the pack needed her strength. In the wake of Caelan's departure, the Silverridge wolves were uncertain. Caelan's intended mate was still a looming presence, a bond that none could ignore, but the truth was that the pack couldn't wait for him to return, couldn't wait for their Alpha to come back to lead them. They needed direction. And Selene was the one who had to give it.

She stood at the head of the pack meeting, her stance resolute as she surveyed the gathered wolves. The air was thick with uncertainty, but it was also heavy with anticipation. They were looking to her now—not as Caelan's Beta, but as their leader. Her heart stuttered at the weight of that responsibility, but she had no time to hesitate. She had to step up, had to take charge.

The voices in the clearing quieted as she raised her hand, signaling the start of the meeting. "Silverridge," she began, her voice carrying through the crisp evening air. "We stand at a crossroads. Many of you have fought beside me, bled for this pack. And now, we move forward together. Not as followers of an Alpha who may or may not return, but as a unified force that will not bend to fate, but instead carve our own path."

Her words were met with a murmur of agreement. She saw it in their eyes—the pack was waiting for her to guide them. No one was looking at her with pity anymore. They were looking to her for strength, for leadership.

"We will rebuild. We will grow stronger," Selene continued. "The fight isn't over. Our enemies are still out there. The rogues who challenge us. The rival packs who would see us fall. But we are Silverridge, and we will stand tall."

One of the younger wolves, a girl named Lyra, spoke up from the crowd, her voice filled with determination. "How will we move forward, Selene? We need direction. We need someone to guide us. The wolves... they don't know where to turn."

Selene nodded, acknowledging the truth of her words. She knew the pack was fragile, fragile in a way that had nothing to do with their strength, but everything to do with their loyalty to Caelan. His absence was felt in every corner of their lives. But it was time for them to find a new way forward.

"We will stay united," Selene answered firmly. "I will take up the mantle, but this isn't my pack alone. It's all of ours. Together, we will decide how we move forward. And if any wolf in this pack has doubts, I'll face them head-on, just as I've always done. We stand as one. As Silverridge."

The wolves exchanged looks—unsure at first, but slowly nodding in agreement. Selene's heart swelled with a mixture of relief and hope. This was the start of something new, something that was hers to shape.

The next few days were filled with difficult decisions. Selene knew she couldn't act alone. She sought out Kael, who had been at her side through the darkest moments, offering advice when she'd needed it most. He had proven to be a valuable ally, a steady presence in the storm that had become her life. But it wasn't just Kael. There were others, too. Old allies from before Caelan's rise to Alpha, those who had once stood at her side, now stepped forward to offer their help. She met with them late into the night, discussing strategy, training schedules, and the state of the pack. There was much to do. The pack had suffered under the weight of its own divisions, but now, for the first time in months, there was a sense of purpose. Together, they would rebuild Silverridge into something stronger, something better.

The following week, Selene called a training session for the warriors—those who had fought alongside her, and those who needed to learn the ways of battle. She stood at the front, her posture strong, her voice commanding.

"Today, we train not for survival, but for dominance," she said. "We train to remind every wolf in the forest that Silverridge is not to be trifled with. We will be stronger than ever before, and we will be ready for whatever comes our way."

Kael stood off to the side, watching her with a proud smile. He had always believed in her potential, in the strength that she possessed, and now, it was clear to everyone that she was capable of far more than they had realized. The wolves were responding to her leadership, training with renewed vigor, following her commands as they never had before.

After the training session, when the wolves were gathered around the fire, resting and recovering from the grueling drills, Selene approached Kael. She felt the weight of his gaze on her, but this time, it wasn't one of pity or sympathy—it was one of pride, and perhaps something more.

"You've done it," Kael said quietly, his voice almost reverent.

"I'm just getting started," Selene replied, her lips curling into a small smile. She had to remind herself that she wasn't finished yet. This was only the beginning. The path ahead was still uncertain, but for the first time in a long time, she felt like she had the power to shape it.

Kael seemed to sense the unspoken promise in her words, and he gave her a knowing look. "Whatever comes next, I'll be here. I've got your back."

"Thank you," she said, her voice soft, but filled with sincerity. "I know I've put you through a lot, Kael, but you've always been there when I needed you."

Kael simply nodded. "You don't need to thank me. I'm not going anywhere."

Selene watched him for a moment, the flickering flames reflecting in his eyes. She wasn't sure what the future held for them—whether Kael would remain by her side in the way he had been or if their paths would diverge in time. But one thing was certain: right now, he was her ally, her friend, and maybe—just maybe—something more.

But even if nothing else ever came of their bond, Selene was ready to walk the path ahead, alone if need be, but never without purpose.

The moon rose high above the Silverridge clearing, casting a pale glow over the pack as they gathered once more. The stars twinkled brightly in the dark sky, a reminder that no matter how lost she had once felt, there was always a way forward.

Selene stood at the head of the pack, looking out at the faces of those she had once called comrades and now called family. The night felt different—charged with energy, with possibility.

"I don't know what the future holds," she said to the pack, her voice firm, filled with conviction. "But I know one thing: we will stand together. We will rise, no matter what. Silverridge will be stronger than ever."

And as the pack erupted in a chorus of cheers and howls, Selene knew in her heart that the path ahead, though unknown, was hers to shape.

No longer bound by the past, she would carve a new future—for herself, for Silverridge, and for every wolf who called the pack home.

The journey had only just begun.

CHAPTER 22: THE HEART'S TRUE CALL

The forest had changed since the first time Selene had found herself standing on this very ground. The familiar trees seemed to whisper old secrets, their leaves rustling with a sound she almost recognized, like the beating of her own heart. She had learned so much in the weeks since Caelan had disappeared. She had learned to lead with strength, with purpose, and to stand tall even when the weight of her past threatened to crush her. But despite all that growth, despite the renewed sense of control she'd gained, there was still something missing.

And it wasn't just the pack.

It was Caelan.

The Alpha of Silverridge had not returned since that fateful night in the clearing. After he'd walked away from her and chosen to honor the prophecy over their bond, Selene had spent her days leading the pack, holding everything together. She had done what was necessary. But her heart, deep down, had never stopped aching for the man she was meant to be with.

The moon hung high in the sky, casting its ethereal glow over the pack territory as Selene stood near the edge of the forest. The night air was crisp, the stars scattered across the sky like a thousand tiny diamonds. She inhaled deeply, allowing the stillness of the night to wash over her. Yet, her mind was anything but still. Her thoughts were tangled, caught in a web of conflicting emotions.

She had spent so much time convincing herself that she was fine without him—that she could move forward, lead the pack, fulfill her purpose without ever needing Caelan again. But the truth was undeniable. Caelan wasn't just her Alpha. He wasn't just the leader of Silverridge. He was her true mate. Her destined mate. The one the stars had carved out for her. Her heart had known it from the very first time she'd met him. She'd felt the pull, the undeniable connection between them, a bond that couldn't be severed by time or distance or betrayal.

And yet, he had left.

Her heart beat faster at the thought of him. She didn't know if he would ever return. Didn't know if he would ever look at her the way he had once before. And even if he did, could she ever forgive him for the pain he'd caused? Could she ever trust him again?

The sound of soft footsteps on the forest floor interrupted her thoughts. She stiffened, instinctively stepping into the shadows, only to see a familiar figure emerge from the trees. Caelan.

For a moment, she stood frozen, heart racing. His presence, even from a distance, sent a shiver through her. He was just as she remembered—tall, broad-shouldered, with dark eyes that seemed to see straight through her. His hair, wild from the wind, was longer now, a few inches past his shoulders, and his expression was softer, less guarded than it had been the last time they had spoken.

"Selene," he said softly, his voice low and hesitant. "I wasn't sure if you'd be here."

"I come here often," she replied, trying to keep her voice steady, her eyes avoiding his. She wasn't sure what she was supposed to feel. Anger? Betrayal? Or was it something else? Something deeper?

Caelan stepped forward, his gaze locked on hers, searching for something. "I—I've been trying to find the right words, the right moment to speak to you," he said. "But I didn't know where to begin."

Selene's pulse quickened. "You left, Caelan. You left without a word, without an explanation."

"I know," he said, his voice filled with remorse. "I never should have walked away from you. I thought I had to honor the prophecy, the bond that the moon had cast between us. But I was wrong, Selene. I was a fool."

Her breath caught at his words. She didn't expect him to say that—not after everything. She expected him to defend his actions, to justify his choices. But he didn't. He was standing here, vulnerable in a way he never had been before.

"I hurt you," he continued, stepping closer, his voice raw. "And I can't take back what I did. But what I've learned over these weeks, what I've realized, is that none of it matters. Not the prophecy, not the bond with her. The only thing that matters is you. You, Selene. You've always been my true mate. My destined mate."

The words hung in the air, heavy and impossible. Selene's heart stuttered in her chest. How could it be so simple? How could he say these things now, after all this time? But as she stood there, staring into his eyes, she felt it. The pull. The undeniable connection. It surged inside her, stronger than it had ever been before.

She was his. And he was hers.

"I don't know if I can trust you again," Selene said, her voice trembling. "I've moved on. I've learned to stand on my own."

"I'm not asking you to forget everything," Caelan said gently, his voice thick with emotion. "I'm not asking you to forgive me overnight. But I'm asking for a chance, Selene. A chance to prove that I'm not the man who abandoned you. I'll fight for you. I'll fight for us."

Tears welled up in her eyes, the flood of emotions she had been suppressing for so long threatening to spill over. She had thought that part of her heart had healed, that it had closed itself off to him, to the past. But standing here, feeling the weight of his words, the sincerity in his gaze, she couldn't help but wonder if maybe, just maybe, there was a chance for them after all.

"I don't know if I can believe you," she said quietly. "But I want to. I want to believe that we can still be what we were meant to be."

Caelan stepped forward again, closing the distance between them until there was no space left, just the quiet night air surrounding them. His hand reached for hers, and Selene didn't pull away. She let him take her hand, their fingers intertwining in a familiar, comforting way.

"I'm not asking for everything right now," he said softly, brushing his thumb across her knuckles. "But can you give me a chance to show you that I can be the man you need? The mate you deserve?"

She looked up at him, her heart beating wildly in her chest, and something deep within her shifted. The walls she had built around herself, the walls that had kept her safe from the pain he'd caused, started to crumble. Maybe she didn't have all the answers yet. Maybe she didn't know how to move forward, but in this moment, she knew one thing for sure. Caelan wasn't the only one who had been searching for the right words. She had been searching for them too.

"I'll try," she whispered, her voice barely a breath. "I'll try, Caelan. But we'll take it one step at a time."

He smiled, a genuine, heartfelt smile that made her chest ache. "That's all I'm asking for."

As they stood there, hand in hand, the moon shining brightly above them, Selene felt the weight of everything she had been carrying finally lift. The pack. Her duty. Her past with Caelan. All of it had led her to this moment. And in this moment, she knew that together, they could face whatever came next. Together, they would rebuild. Together, they would lead.

And as their lips met in a soft, tentative kiss, Selene knew that she had made the right choice. No matter what the future held, she was ready to face it by Caelan's side.

The journey ahead would be difficult, but it would be theirs. Together.

EPILOGUE: A NEW BEGINNING

A year had passed since Selene and Caelan had stood together in the forest, each unsure of what their future might look like. The Silverridge pack had grown in ways they hadn't anticipated. Under Selene's leadership, and with Caelan by her side, they had faced challenges, healed old wounds, and reclaimed their rightful place as one of the most powerful packs in the region. But it wasn't just the pack that had flourished; Selene and Caelan, too, had grown stronger, not just as leaders, but as a couple. As true mates.

The sun was setting over the forest, casting long shadows over the valley where the pack had made their home. Selene stood at the edge of the cliff, her eyes watching the horizon. The breeze tangled her dark hair, and the cool evening air felt like a balm against the heat of the day. She closed her eyes for a moment, letting the peace of the world around her settle in her bones. It had been a long road, full of pain and doubt, but now, standing here, she felt nothing but serenity.

Her heart had healed. Not just because of the pack, but because of Caelan.

He had kept his promise. The journey they had walked together hadn't been easy, and there were times when Selene had wondered if they would ever find their way back to one another fully. But each day, each step they took, brought them closer. Caelan had earned back her trust, and in the quiet moments between the chaos of their leadership, she had found herself falling in love with him again. Not just the Alpha he had been, but the man who loved her, who cherished her, who had never truly left her side, even when he had walked away.

The pack had flourished as well. They were no longer a fractured, divided group, torn between loyalty to an absent Alpha and the need for leadership. Now, they stood united, under Selene and Caelan's guidance. They had reclaimed what had once been lost, and together, they were building something new, something stronger than they had ever imagined.

"Selene?" The familiar voice, low and warm, broke through her thoughts. She turned, her heart skipping a beat at the sight of Caelan walking toward her, his tall figure framed by the fading light. His eyes, those dark eyes that had once been clouded with doubt and confusion, now radiated clarity and certainty. He was no longer the man who had abandoned her. He was the man who had chosen her, over and over again, despite the odds.

"I thought I'd find you here," he said, his voice filled with quiet affection.

"I come here to think," she replied, offering him a small smile. "Sometimes, I need a moment of silence to remember how far we've come."

Caelan reached her side, standing just a few feet away, his gaze drifting toward the horizon as well. The years had not dimmed the strength of his presence, nor the power of their connection. In fact, it only seemed to grow with time. He was no longer just the Alpha of Silverridge; he was her mate, her partner, the man who had made her whole again.

"I know what you mean," he said after a moment of silence. "There were times when I didn't think we'd get here. When I thought I'd lost you for good."

Selene's heart clenched at the sincerity in his voice. She knew. She had felt the same way. But now, standing beside him, she realized how far they had both come. They had fought through their past together, faced the darkness that had once threatened to tear them apart, and come out stronger for it. Their bond had never truly been broken, no matter how much they'd tried to fight it.

"I thought we had lost everything," she said softly, her eyes reflecting the sunset. "But in the end, it brought us back to each other."

Caelan's hand reached for hers, his touch warm and familiar. "I never stopped loving you, Selene. And I never will."

A smile tugged at her lips, and for a moment, she felt a rush of gratitude for the man beside her. He wasn't perfect—no one was—but he had proven, time and again, that his love for her was unwavering. And in the end, that was all that mattered.

Together, they had built something new. A future. A life that was theirs to shape.

The wind picked up again, swirling around them as they stood there in comfortable silence. It was a reminder of how much had changed and yet how much had stayed the same. They were still the same two people who had met under the full moon, two souls destined to be together. But now, they were stronger. They had learned to lead with love, with compassion, and with trust.

"I was thinking," Caelan said, breaking the silence once more. "We've come so far. Maybe it's time for the pack to take the next step. To truly establish ourselves as more than just a group of wolves, but as a family. A place where everyone belongs."

Selene's eyes sparkled with the same fire that had always been in her heart. "You're right. We've done more than rebuild the pack; we've created something lasting. Something that can endure."

Caelan's eyes softened as he looked at her, and Selene felt the pull of their bond once again, as if the universe itself was telling them they were where they were meant to be.

"Then let's make it official," he said, his voice filled with certainty. "Let's show the world what Silverridge really stands for."

With a smile, Selene nodded. "We will."

Weeks later, Silverridge saw its greatest transformation. The pack, under the leadership of Selene and Caelan, had not only become a unified force but also a beacon of strength and resilience. They had forged alliances with neighboring packs, helped to heal the wounds of old rivalries, and established Silverridge as a place of peace and unity in the werewolf world.

Selene had become more than just the Alpha's mate. She had become a leader in her own right—tough, compassionate, and wise beyond her years. She and Caelan led together, their partnership strengthening the pack and forging a new future for them all.

The night of the full moon, under the same sky that had witnessed their bond forming, Selene and Caelan stood before the pack. The firelight flickered in their eyes as they prepared to announce something they had both been working toward for months.

"We've come a long way," Caelan said, his voice carrying across the gathered wolves. "But we're not done yet. Tonight, we stand together, as one family. The future of Silverridge belongs to all of us. And together, we will rise."

Selene stood beside him, her heart full. The pack cheered, howls echoing into the night. And in that moment, Selene knew that the pack's journey was far from over—but now, they were all in this together.

She had her mate. She had her pack. And for the first time in a long time, Selene felt the weight of the world lift from her shoulders. She was exactly where she was meant to be. Together with Caelan. Together with the pack.

And together, they would face whatever the future held.

The moon shone brightly overhead, casting its glow across Silverridge. The sound of wolves howling echoed through the night, signaling a new beginning. And as Selene and Caelan stood hand in hand, their hearts aligned, they knew that no matter what came next, they were ready. They had fought for this moment, and now, with the love of their pack and each other, they would build a future that would last for generations.

The future of Silverridge was theirs. The future of their love was theirs. And together, they would lead the way.

The end of one chapter was only the beginning of another.